folk music

Also by Sheenagh Pugh

Poetry
Beware Falling Tortoises
Selected Poems
Sing for the Taxman
Id's Hospit
Stonelight

Translations
Prisoners of Transience

Sheenagh Pugh
folk music

seren

seren is the book imprint of
Poetry Wales Press Ltd
Wyndham Street, Bridgend, CF31 1EF, Wales

ISBN 1-85411-268-6

A CIP record for this title is available from
the British Library

*The publisher works with the financial assistance of the
Arts Council of Wales*

Printed in Plantin by CPD Wales, Ebbw Vale

folk music

To Michael

1

THE SINGER

There's always one face you sing to. One that looks brighter, that speaks to you more than the rest do. You pick her out of the crowd – well it's a her with me, anyway, and a young pretty her at that. I'm only human. And then all the words you sing that night are for her.

I'm tired tonight; I've had a long journey and I don't really feel like singing; if it weren't for the money I'd as soon go to bed. They bring me into the room and it's just a blur of faces and voices; I'm being greeted and trying not to yawn; then someone gives me some wine, which helps a bit, but on top of the tiredness it goes to my head. I'm just sitting there, sipping and looking, when all of a sudden it comes over me that I'm staring straight at the married women, or at least at the big dark eyes above their veils. I only realise what I'm doing when one of them looks down and another giggles.

So I turn away, to where most of the noise is coming from, a group of young girls. They never stop talking, though I suppose you can't blame them. They make out to be thinking of nothing but doing each other's hair, or playing with the cats, but of course every minute, their eyes are sliding over to the boys, and you can see how everything they do is aimed.

They're fussing over a litter of kittens; one girl picks a little tabby up and starts crooning a nursery song to it: Puss, chase the mouse, to his little house.... She's got a good voice, dark and full, so I come in with some harmony and she smiles at me. White teeth, deep red lips; they use berry juice to get that rosebud look, though they'll never admit it. I love girls' mouths. The girl I picked out here last year was all right in that department, but mostly I remember her hair. There was a red tinge to it in the firelight; it was October then, and the colour made me think of a rowan tree in the sun. She isn't here this time; I've already had a quick look round. Dead or wed, as they say; it's either one or the other and I never like to ask.

Redlips'll do to sing to, tonight. I'm waking up a bit:

Throw a letter
into the sky.
The crane's a wanderer;
so am I.

And they join the refrain; always start with something they know, something easy to sing along with. The men deep, coming in a bit ragged; the young lads timid, because they aren't sure if their voices'll come out deep or high. The children, breaking off their game to join in, feeling important because they've been let stay up late. Even the married women swaying, rocking their babies with the rhythm, and their veils stirring ever so slightly as they breathe the words behind them. But the girls are the stars. They all come in perfectly together, because their eyes are fixed on me. I can do that to girls when I sing; it's like I've got them all on threads. I lock eyes with them all, at one time or another, and each one thinks I'm singing for her. The wanderer, who sends letters but no forwarding address; who doesn't stay. *I could make him stay.* That's what they're all thinking. Tame the crane. But then he won't be a crane any more.

Come the autumn,
what flies must fly.
The crane's a wanderer....

Dear God, they're all so beautiful. All that passion and thoughtfulness in their faces, all that feeling for the words. Maybe every girl is beautiful when she sings. Redlips picks up another kitten, black this time; strokes it into a trance against her breast. Lucky bloody kitten. It's almost hidden in her hair; black curls down to the waist. I sign to her to start the next verse; she won't mind. They're not shy, these girls.

Left what I had,
and I don't know why....

She does it splendidly; slow, sad, a bit husky, really acting it. Not for me though. As she throws her curls back, her glance slides over to the young men and – I was going to say, rests on one, but there's nothing restful about how she looks at him; it's like sun burning glass. It's a *you're mine* look – or maybe *I'm yours*: I'm never sure which is scarier.

And I think about the rowan-haired girl last year, and how her eyes laughed back at me. She might be here again next year, I'll never know. Hair can be any colour, under those veils; mouths too. And one pair of dark eyes looks much like another. But I know where she probably is now; so do you, Redlips. If she lives in this house, that is. If she doesn't, she won't have come at all: a bride goes out twice in the first year, both times to church.... But if she lives here, where is she now? On the stairs, in the kitchen, listening to what sounds she can catch? In the room she shares with her husband, waiting for him to come back? She would have slipped out as the stranger came in – if I hadn't been so tired, maybe I'd just have caught a glint of silver from all those ornaments on her dress. The dress you can't wait to wear, Redlips.

Give it a few more years, I want to say; give it for ever. I can hear her voice in the refrain, soaring, unleashed. Who clips a crane and puts it in the barnyard?

But I'm the crane, not them. They like to sing about it; folk with roofs over their heads always like to sing about being on the road. They just wouldn't *do* it, any more than I'd stay put.

Your bread is tasteless,
your water's dry.
The crane's a wanderer,
so am I.

Sing on, Redlips. The way I'm feeling now, this could turn into a long night. But tomorrow I'll wake up with a wrecked throat, gargle with milk and then on to wherever's hired me next. And by the time I get there, I'll be fit to sing again. Six months or so, I'll be singing here again. But you might not, if things go as you want them to.

You've shaken your hair back, and the way your breast

moves as you sing, it's as well I know the words by heart. Your whole being is caught up in the music; you aren't even thinking of *him* any more, just doing what you know you do so well. What comes naturally. And it might be the last night you ever do it. The one you look back on, when you're old. *I was great that night.* It sends shivers down me, just to think of it; every time your voice soars, it's like a thorn going into my heart, and I wouldn't swap the pain for anything....

Enjoy tonight, girl; I'll spin it out as long as I can for you.

Goodbye, my love;
goodbye, goodbye.
The crane's a wanderer...

2

HANNA

"Ow!"

"Stay still, then. I can't help getting pins in you if you move."

But I'd got her facing away from the mirror, and she couldn't leave it alone; she kept craning over her shoulder, half-turning to see the long silk panels, silver on rose-pink. She did a quick swish to see how they moved, just as I was trying to alter a dart. Pins all over the floor.

"Sorry." She looked as sorry as a bird in spring. I called Ria. "Come and pick these pins up for me; I can't let go of this." And she came dawdling over.

"Why can't *she* do it?" Why does no-one ever do anything willingly, or without an argument?

"Because she can't move either; can't you see that for yourself? Just do it, please."

"It's not fair; you never talk to *her* like that." She started on the pins, making up a song as she did it:

My big sister's getting wed,
when she's gone, I'll have her bed.

"You sing like a frog. Or like Dad."

"At least I'll be *able* to sing, this time next week. And talk. To anyone I like. Except you, of course"

"That'll be a relief, anyway. A bit of peace and quiet at last. I can hardly wait."

"Stop it, both of you." I hate to hear them go on like that. And then I thought: next week I'll wish it back.

I fitted the long sleeveless coat, crusted with silver embroidery, over the dress. She twirled the silver ribbons that hung from the collar, and her eyes smiled at me, just like her father's. She's so beautiful. I like her better in her everyday dress; a face like hers doesn't need all that glitter to set it off.

But of course she thought she never looked so good.

"You look" – I hesitated – "really nice."

"*Really nice*," mimicked Ria, "you're always saying things like that to *her*."

Not true. I hadn't said anything like that to her for too long. You forget to, when people are there all the time. The number of days we must have pottered about the same room, with nothing to say... Or the times we fell out, and she'd be watching me across the room, keeping her words back out of anger, and I'd be thinking how sulky she was, as if I weren't just as bad....

When she was first born, I talked and sang to her so much, I lost my voice. Hilarious, eh? My mother-in-law thought so, anyway; she laughed until she cried. I couldn't stop, even then. I was croaking lullabies. "Hush, my Anni, hush, my pet." Mind, I had a good voice in those days, when I hadn't sung myself hoarse, that is. Even from behind a veil it didn't sound too fuzzy. You soon get used to leaning forward a bit and not breathing in too much as you talk or sing, so as not to get the thing in your mouth. Lord, when did I last sing? Not softly, under my breath, as we do in front of strangers: I mean out loud, the way you sing on your own or to a small child? My youngest's twelve – seven years ago, maybe?

Last night, when we were listening to the singer, I caught myself wondering, once or twice, what it would be like to really sing out. But that's like wanting to be young again, to wear your hair open and paint your mouth with berry juice and flirt with the boys; it's just silly. You do that when it's your time to, and then you watch your daughters do it. That's where your pride goes. Anni sings so well, so well... she gets the good looks from her father, but the voice is from our side. My Marti can't hold a tune for the life of him, poor man; he really does sing like a frog. Ria isn't really so bad... in a year or so, when her voice has deepened and filled out a bit....

While I was trying to check the hang of the pleats, her kitten got interested in the glittery bits at the hem and started playing with them. I tried to shoo him, but she stooped and picked him up.

"Hold still... and don't let him put his claws in anything."

"He wouldn't, would you, love? No.... They had lots of pretty kitties where I was last night, but none of them was as nice as you; no, they weren't...." She rubbed noses with him and scratched behind his ears until he purred. Ria was petting him too; they agree about cats, at least.

Some men would have sulked about having two daughters first, but not my Marti. Whenever his mother started on about how lucky her sister was: *three grandsons already; I don't suppose I'll ever see one*, he always stuck up for me. *The sons'll come if they're meant to, and if it's all daughters I'll be just as pleased.* He was always good about taking my side; never let her come first from the day we married. But it's true too that he really does set store by the girls; even after Stevi and Nico came, he was still just as fond of them. He'll miss her a lot.

"All right, walk for me now. Let me see how it hangs." And she did walk, for a few steps, but soon she was gliding, twirling, dancing. I tried to catch at one of the pleats as she passed, and missed.

"Stop a minute, something isn't right." She laughed and spun away, waltzing with the kitten in her arms.

No use for the sun; no use for the south wind,
till he comes through my gate...

"Hold still, you want it to be perfect, don't you?" And she did, but while I was re-pinning it her feet were tapping under the hem, dying to be off. Ria eyed the silver embroidery on the coat, the intricate jewelled collar, the rose-coloured folds of the dress weighted down at the hem with more silver, and snorted.

"Catch me getting that excited about a stupid dress. Or a stupid man." But she couldn't take her eyes off it.

"I think it's right, now. Take it off and I'll finish the sewing."

"Shouldn't I try the veil as well?"

"Oh, there's plenty of time for that. Let's just get on with the dress for now."

"No, I want Dad to see it first. And Bapa." She was off,

with me after her in case the pins came out. "Dad! Bapa! Look at me!"

They were in the garden, drinking coffee. She ran up to them and gave them a twirl. I hadn't seen the outfit in sunlight before; when she spun round, the silver coat shivered and glittered like the fountain. Marti jumped up and hugged her.

"Don't you look beautiful! I've never seen you look so beautiful. I've never seen anyone look so beautiful in a bride's dress – except your mother, of course."

"It's still pinned up, Marti... don't swing her round like that, it'll be in pieces again... ah, careful...."

He put her down, reluctantly, and turned to the old man. "Isn't she lovely, Dad?" He spoke loud and clear, as always, but the old man hardly hears a thing; he nods and smiles when people talk to him, but I think it's only to spare their embarrassment; he hates asking them to repeat things all the time. She knelt down in front of him and spoke slowly, looking straight at him: "Do you like my wedding dress, Bapa?"

She says he can make out more words like that, and his smile did look different; not watery and vague but as if he knew what was going on. He stroked her hair and murmured: "Beautiful... beautiful." His hand rested on her head a while, and he asked: "How long to the wedding?"

"Just a week now," she said happily, and he understood and nodded. He didn't look too happy, but she was already off and twirling again. I wonder if it's dawned on her that five years is a long time at his age. By the time she's allowed to speak to him again, he might not be here.

"Anni, please, I need the dress to work on. Come and take it off now." She waved goodbye to them; bowed in the doorway, like a singer milking the last applause from his audience. Marti laughed proudly, and the old man gazed after her as long as she was in sight.

Ria had to help me get it off intact; there were so many pins in it. We all three got stabbed once or twice, but while Ria shrieked and complained bitterly each time, Anni never stopped singing for a moment.

14

See that girl dressed all in yellow,
she's so mad 'cos she wants my fellow,
see that girl dressed all in red,
she's so mad, she wants me dead.

Ria raised her eyes to heaven. "I don't know how much more of this hilarity I can stand.... Still not long now. Blessed peace." Anni made a face at her.

See that girl dressed all in blue,
got no man, but she can't have you.

Ria yawned. "You don't need me any more, do you? Good." She wandered off, and a moment later we heard her voice outside, with Stevi and Nico and their friends. Anni laughed and changed the tune.

Come down, come down, you pretty little bird,
come down out of the tree.
I'll give you berries from my hand,
and a cage of ivory.

"Don't move; that daft dog's got his paw on the hem.... Off, now; there's a good lad.... Look, she *is* right, you know; in a week it's all going to be different. No more singing, no chatting with your mates, no arguing with Ria. You should think about it."

"I thought you wanted me to get married! It's a bit flaming late to change your mind, isn't it?"

"I don't mean that; everyone needs someone of their own, and Andras is a nice lad. I'm saying you don't have a clue what it's going to be like, and it isn't as easy as you think – I've done it, remember. Going to *his* house, never leaving it for the first year except for church, staying out of sight when strangers call, never seeing your kin unless they come to visit..."

"Well, you can, can't you?"

"Yes we can, but it isn't the same as what she just did, going out to spend time with her brothers because she felt like it. You might not have spent much time with them lately, being wrapped up in Andras, but that's different from not being able to. And seeing isn't talking, either."

"I *know* all that."

"No, you know *about* it, that's all."

She tossed her hair back, angrily. "The way you talk, I wonder you ever married Dad!"

"Don't be silly."

"But that's what I mean... anyone can see you're happy," She twisted a curl round one finger; funny how she's always done that when she was nervous about something. "You *are* happy, aren't you? And you wouldn't have done any different? It's all worthwhile?"

"Yes, it was all worthwhile."

"Well, then... I feel just the same about Andras. I'm prepared for all that stuff."

Never, I thought. I could still hear Ria, laughing and joking with the lads outside, and for a moment I thought: I wonder if it's such a good idea to give our girls so much freedom. Wearing what they like, mixing with the lads, choosing their own husbands. It's fine while it lasts, but when they have to lose it...

Anni caught one particular voice in the crowd, and ran to the window.

"Hey, Edo! What are you doing hanging around with the kids?"

He smiled back at her; a tall, gangly lad who looked even more awkward among boys five or six years younger. "Just keeping an eye on my brothers. You sang great last night."

"Yeah, didn't I? Want to see the dress?" She held it up to the window, but his sad eyes never left her face. They nearly always were sad, though not usually when he was talking to her. She waved, and turned back into the room, singing under her breath.

"Edo isn't... in love with you, is he?"

"*Edo*? Lord, no. He doesn't feel that way about anyone. It's just he likes talking to me. He's never got on with the lads much, you know; they tease him because he's quiet. He gets lonely, and he needs someone to listen to him. I'm just the one he likes to pour things out to."

Poor Edo, I thought. But what I said was: "Just get on and have that first baby as soon as you can. It'll be good to hear you sing to it."

3

ANDRAS

I was shattered after work; we all were. We seemed to be moving hides between pits, or rolling them, or stacking them for drying, all day. And then late on, a whole new batch of market hides came in, all over blood and muck and heavy as hell. By the time Marti said we could knock off, I was aching all over, especially my shoulders and stomach, where I'd strained it using the roller.

Some of us went down to the river for a quick wash. The water was so cold it felt painful where we ached; the spring sun was low already and it didn't seem to have warmed anything. Jos was so stiff, he couldn't reach his back with his hands. I dried it for him, and gave his shoulders a rub.

"Oh, God, thanks, mate. You coming down the Eagle after?"

"No, not tonight. I'm going over Anni's."

"Well, there's a surprise. Come on, she could do without you one night a week, surely? Some of the lads are going into town later; we might get a lift."

"No, I promised her. I'll come another time."

"Bloody hell. I hope I never get that much in love. Oh, that feels great... Do you want me to do yours now?"

"I'm OK, thanks. See you tomorrow."

Some of the other lads looked a bit sideways when I left. They think I feel bound to spend so much time with her, because Marti's the boss. Jos knows it isn't like that, but even he thinks it's odd for me to want to be with her so much, instead of the lads.

I can't help that. I don't feel like one of the lads any more. The last couple of times I was out with them, I just couldn't concentrate on it or see what I'd ever liked about it. They were on about the match, and the girls they reckoned they'd been with, and how much they'd drunk the night before, and I couldn't have cared less. I wanted to be with her; listen to her giving me the gossip about her girlfriends or singing to her kitten.

It's a bit embarrassing when I have to walk back with Marti though, not that I've got anything against him; as bosses go he's great, but he's still the boss and there's always someone who'll give you that look: *you did all right didn't you, getting off with the boss's daughter.* But he stayed on late this time, so I went on my own. When I was still yards from her door, I could hear her singing.

It was Ria who answered the door. She took a look at me and raised one eyebrow.

"Oh, it's God Almighty."

She called through to the inner room: "It's Andras, folks; who would have thought it?" and led me inside. Anni's mother was there with the lads. She shook her head at Ria.

"Your manners get worse by the day, really they do. What sort of way is that to speak to a guest?"

"'Tisn't a guest, it's only Andras... I'll just nip up and tell the faithful he's manifested himself."

She disappeared up the stairs, and I smiled, a bit hesitantly, at Anni's mother. She's got kind eyes; they always made me feel her mouth was smiling too, behind the veil. But they'd started looking sad sometimes lately, and I wondered if she didn't like Anni marrying me. I wished I could ask her if it was anything I'd done. I turned to the boys instead.

"How's school?"

"Lousy", said Stevi, with some feeling, "the sooner I'm done with it the better. It all goes in one ear and out the other, I'm that bored."

"How do you expect to amount to anything", his mother protested in her soft voice that just wasn't designed for effective nagging, "if you won't take an interest in learning?"

"I want to *work*, not learn; why can't I work in the yard with Dad? Andras does."

"Well, no offence to your dad, Stevi, but I'm not doing it because I like it; it's a job, and a fairly smelly, filthy, back-breaking one at that. You've seen the state your dad and me are in when we get home; don't you fancy coming home clean from an office and feeling fit to see your girlfriend?"

"How come *you* couldn't wait to get out of school and into the yard, then?" God, there's nothing like kids for asking awkward questions.

"I don't know. Because I was as daft as you, I expect."

"Of course," his mother said quietly, "it could be that Andras wanted to make life easier for his mother. Grown men don't do just as they like, as if they were still children."

The boys made halo signs, and I'd have been dead embarrassed, normally, but her eyes gave me that warm look again; as if she knew I was worried about what she thought of me, and I felt so grateful. I wanted to thank her, but I couldn't think of a way of saying it through the boys. And then it all went out of my head, because I heard Anni singing behind me.

Your mind is shallow, they say;
so too your love,
but oh, that beautiful face...
What was God thinking of?

And there she was on the bottom step, her face glowing, and I ran to her and she jumped down into my arms. The boys were going "yuk", and Ria whistling derisively, and I was just so happy to be with her, I forgot how much I was aching until she squeezed my shoulders and I yelled.

"Oh poor love, are they stiff again? Sit on the couch."

She stood behind me, kneading my shoulders and neck with her fingers, and even though she was scared of hurting me and didn't do it hard enough, it was so relaxing. I closed my eyes. The river hadn't changed anything much, but her touch and her voice felt like they were washing the tannin out of my hands, the smell of lime out of my hair, and the ache out of my bones. The tanyard didn't exist, nor the lads down the Eagle, nor Ria and the boys still joking somewhere on the edge of my hearing. I couldn't think of anything except her, and loving her.

In a while, she took me out to the garden. It wasn't like being alone, naturally, because it was a courtyard overlooked from all sides, and of course we always had to leave the doors open. But we loved being able to talk without being overheard; we'd sit by the fountain to cover our chat, in case one of the boys sneaked up. Anni's mother generally stopped them, though.

"I've been thinking about you all day. I could hardly keep my mind on the job."

"Well, don't tell Dad that. I don't fancy starting married life with you out of work."

"Don't you think about me during the day, then?"

"Course I do. All the time, when I can't see you. I even have conversations with you in my mind. Sometimes I'm talking to Mum, or Ria, and I'll say the wrong thing, because I've got mixed up with what I'm saying to you inside my head."

"Ria's always so sarky to me these days. We used to get on all right."

Anni shrugged. "She doesn't like me being so wrapped up in you, but I can't do anything about that, can I?" She rubbed her face against my shoulder, like a kitten, and my hand clenched on hers so much that she cried out softly.

"Oh, I'm sorry! I didn't mean to hurt you. Are you all right?" I stroked her hand and kissed it; it smelled of orange-flowers. She always did. Whenever I smelled her perfume, I felt something almost like pain. She just smiled and nodded, and I let go of her hand because I was in such a turmoil I was dead scared I'd hurt her again. It looked so small and fragile beside mine. And so white; even my palms were dark with ingrained tannin. It seemed all wrong that I should ever touch her at all. I put my hands under the fountain and let them cool. There was a bird singing nearby; I could see it in a bush, singing its heart out, really throbbing with the effort. I couldn't believe its body could hold all that sound.

"It's so little. Do you think it hurts them, singing?"

She thought about it. "No... no, how could it? He's happy."

"I think happiness hurts, sometimes." There was a patch of colour under his bush; bluebells. I bent over and tilted the bell of one upwards with my finger, feeling how frail the stem was. The bird sang right on, even with me so near. I could see now that the bush was full of long, wicked thorns; I couldn't think

21

how he'd got so deep in without getting torn.

There was a sort of merry commotion from the house, and I knew Marti must be home. I put my arm around her, feeling as if I had hold of that bird in the bush, and we went back indoors. She ran to him and cuddled him, looking tiny against his barrel chest, then brushed the dust off his coat. He stroked her hair and laughed, and then it turned into a cough.

"You've been grinding bark. Shall I get you some water?"

"It's all right, your mother's gone for it. You fuss over Andras."

She turned back to me. "You haven't been grinding it too, have you? I didn't see the dust on you."

"No, I was shifting hides all day." She buried her face on my shoulder for a moment and announced triumphantly: "In the lime-pits." Then she caught up my hand and smelt it. "And a bit of cod-liver oil; you must have been oiling them for stacking." It was a game with her; she always reckoned she could tell what work Marti'd been doing that day in the yard, and when we started courting she did it with me as well.

Anni's mother came back with the water, in a big tankard, and Marti downed it in one and smiled gratefully at her. "You're magic, you; you always know just what I need."

"I should, by now." She moved around the table, getting the supper things set out. Whenever she came near Marti's chair he'd take her hand for an instant, or she'd stroke his hair in passing. If Anni and I'd done that, the boys would have been mouthing "soppy" or making sick noises, but I don't think they even noticed it with those two; it just seemed so natural.

I liked having supper at Anni's place. I liked it when she came round our place too, but there was a different atmosphere in our house, because my mother had been a widow so long. Not that she was a misery or anything; she got on with life whatever happened, and she was very good about Anni, didn't seem to resent her or try to hang on to me. But for the life of me, I couldn't remember Mum and my dad together – couldn't remember him at all, much – and whenever I saw Anni's folks I used to wonder if mine had been like that, and wish I could have known it.

Anni'd gone upstairs to wake her grandfather and bring him down for supper. That was the one drawback about her place – oh, that sounds horrible, I don't mean it like that. He was a nice old man, and Anni was very fond of him; if I hadn't treated him right, she'd never have given me the time of day. And I liked him, I really did, but it was murder to get anything across to him. You'd have to say it over and over, even the simplest little thing, and every time it seemed more pointless and more embarrassing. And I'd find myself not meeting his eye, getting engrossed in talk with someone else, just to avoid the problem, and then I'd feel so ashamed. I wasn't the only one, either; it was so easy, when folk were chatting a lot, to forget he was there and suddenly you'd become aware of him, like a little island. Anni didn't let that happen, usually, but sometimes when we were together, neither of us noticed anyone else much. There were usually about three different conversations going on at that table anyway.

I remember that night, she was telling me about the wedding dress and I was nodding every so often, and suddenly she stopped and clapped her hands sharply in front of my face.

"You're not listening to a word I'm saying, are you?"

"No, not really." She threw her hands in the air, and I said: "I could hear your voice; I was sitting back enjoying the sound of it. I just didn't notice what it was saying." I ducked her hand, and it brushed past my ear.

"What's that for? I was attending to you, honest; it's just that I don't care what your voice says as long as I can hear it. I was looking at your eyes and thinking how they sparkle when you're excited about something. It didn't matter what."

She aimed another mock-slap at me and looked pleased, and Marti laughed, but her mother's eyes looked worried again. It troubled me for a moment, and I started listening to the terrible jokes Stevi and Nico were swapping, to take my mind off it. And soon I was groaning, and laughing in spite of myself, and sliding my eyes over to Anni as she and her mother nattered on about the dress again. And Ria would notice our eyes meet, and make some spiky comment, and Marti'd shush her as if he were angry, grinning all the while, because she was bright, Ria; you couldn't deny it. I leaned back in my chair, feeling pure happiness.

And there he was, on the edge of my vision, his eyes moving from one face to another and reading none of them; his expression still, unmoved; calm amidst a storm of talk and laughter: the little white island.

4

BAPA

I know more of what's going on than they think. When you can't hear, you notice other things more – people's faces, for instance, when they have to talk to you. I can read impatience, embarrassment and blind panic very well.

I sound bitter. I shouldn't, really. My son and daughter-in-law do their best – he bellows as loud as he can, in case it makes a difference, and it does; it feels as if there's a storm at sea inside my ears and I can't make out a thing. And she talks with her hands and eyes, or uses pictures and objects; she must feel, sometimes, as if she's gone back to being first married. She gets a lot more across to me that way. I should be grateful, and sometimes I am. But other times, it panics me, the thought that she's stopped even trying to reach me with sound. I feel as if I'm drifting away.

A day like this, I feel it more. When it's an Occasion; when everyone's together and I'm not part of it. There, but not part of it. I'm watching it, as if it were happening behind glass; people meeting, talking, throwing back their heads and laughing, and now and again someone'll think to tell me what's being said. And by the time it gets across to me, they've moved on to something else.

Normally the lass would spend more time with me, but I can't really expect it today. She looks beautiful in that dress. It's strange not to see her hair, now she's got the head-veil on; I'm so used to seeing her shake her curls back, or twist her fingers in them. It's all covered, now. But she hasn't got the other part on yet, so I can still see her mouth, laughing. She speaks so clear and slow to me; I can read her lips better than anyone's.

They've sat me in the shade, among the old men with their lizardy skin, all brown and wrinkled and hanging in flaps under the chin, and we're all eyeing each other and thinking: surely I don't look like that? Not so dried-out and milky-eyed; not sour like Marko, nor vacant like Theo with his permanent misplaced grin? I remember when you couldn't keep the girls off him. We don't want to look at each other; our eyes keep stealing glances, then edging off elsewhere. I'm looking at that little wood in the far distance; I can't see to read any more, but the farther off things are, the clearer they get. That makes me panic too, when I think about it. The floor of that wood is all a bluish haze, but that's no fault of my eyesight; it's covered with bluebells at this time of year. I used to bring them back for Kati. She loved blue things – sparrows' eggs, myrtle berries, hyacinths; I'd bring her the bulbs to plant in the garden.

Young Tomas – young, he must be fifty – comes and gives me the time of day, I suppose. He could be proposing we blow up the government for all I know, but I smile and nod; it wouldn't be such a bad plan anyway. *He's* all right, but that wife of his, the lemon-faced bitch, is talking to my daughter-in-law, and you only have to look at her narrow eyes, and Hanna lowering hers, to know she's saying something spiteful. I wish I knew what; *I'd* have an answer quick enough. But Hanna has to think, collect herself, and then she just says something quiet and turns away.

She's a gentle woman, always was, and never the sort who had an answer ready at her tongue's end. When Marti first started courting her, I was inclined to think of her as nice but vapid – I'd always preferred a girl with a bit of salt, like my Kati. But then when they married, I really missed her voice. Not just her singing voice, though she'd been famous for that. It was more her speaking voice; very low and warm, almost like someone humming music, and it made you feel more at ease somehow. All that year, I went about short of temper, feeling there was something astray about the house, and then when the baby was born and I heard her crooning to it, I knew it was her voice I'd been missing.

It was another three years, of course, before she could talk to me, but long before then I'd hear her chatting to Marti and Kati, and then later the other women in the house, and it always made me feel as if I were sitting in the sun. I daresay it was partly *what* she said, or didn't say; she never seemed to nag or scold and if there was ever a quarrel she'd be trying to settle it. But I think it was mainly just the sound of her voice. I suppose it still sounds like that.

She looks happier now; she's chatting to young Andras's mother. Dear God, how long ago was I at *her* wedding? She must have been a widow almost as long as Anni's been alive – longer than the lads, for sure – and yet I recall her as a young girl. Emmi, her name was. Very lively; plenty to say for herself, not unlike my Kati when she was young. She even went out with one of Marti's brothers for a while, but it didn't come to anything.

I can see her sliding her eyes across to me, thinking: he'll be family in an hour or so and I'll have to try to talk to him. Oh, maybe not; I must stop thinking like this or I'll end up looking as vinegary as Marko. She always got on all right with me when she was a girl. It'll be strange to speak to her again after all these years. I wonder what my voice sounds like now. Sometimes when I speak, people start, or take a step back, so I think maybe it's louder outside than it seems in my head. Or maybe they're just amazed I still *can* speak. I don't think they know deaf from daft, half of them.

Every so often, there's a brief dazzle of white light from the edge of my vision, where Anni is. She only has to stir, and the sun flashes off all that silver. Young Andras can't forget it's there either; he's quite close to me, chatting to his mates, but every time she does a twirl I can see his eyes wander. He isn't listening to the talk, I can see – I know what he looks like when he's concentrating. The poor lad came over when he first arrived and made heroic efforts to talk to me for about ten minutes. I'd be staring intently at his lips, and they'd make shapes I couldn't read, and he'd make the same shapes again.... In the end, I let on to be sleepy, because I felt sorry for him. He really loves the lass anyway, and that's what matters. I used to be aware of Kati like that. I might be talking to someone else, even looking at them, but if she came in or went out, I knew.

The white light's moving. Anni's started to go the rounds, saying goodbye. The gaggle of girls she's with, first. They've gone much quieter now; she hugs each in turn, floods of tears all round, and each one says something. I can guess: good luck; won't seem long; soon be chatting again... It's all very well for them; what's a few years at that age?

Then the young men go over, leaving Andras on his own, and they wish her luck too. And this is different, more serious, despite the lack of tears, because unless they get to be related by blood or marriage, they might never hear her voice again, except when it's speaking to someone else. They all look grave, a bit sad; she's always been popular. Christ, that Edo's nearly crying; do something about the snivelling wretch, someone, before he causes a scene... She holds his hands in her own and says something. He smiles, uncertainly, but at least he's back in control, just; he looks as much of a man as he ever will. There's something odd about that Edo, if you ask me. He's never been part of the gang, always on the edge of things; it's not natural. Don't know why she has so much patience with him. Had.

Now she moves away, circling a bit; she knows what it does to that dress, and starts coming round the relatives. Cousins, aunties, uncles; I can't recall who half of them are. It used to seem so important to keep track, at least of the women, so I knew who I was allowed to speak direct to and who I had to talk to through someone else. But they're all the same now. Then Stevi and Nico, no jokes for once, and Ria's got nothing much to say, which must be a first. They tell me she's as quick as my Kati was.

Me now. She comes and kneels in front of me, and looks straight into my eyes. The first set of shapes she makes, I can't read, so she changes the words:

"Be happy, Bapa. I'll miss you."

"Me too." I wish I knew what my voice sounded like. "Bless you; be happy."

"I'll come and have a long talk again as soon as I can." Well, that's something to look forward to; I'll keep it in mind, any time the next five years happen to drag a bit. She hugs me, and I stroke what ought to be her hair, but is of course her silk veil, smooth and flat where I'm used to her springy curls.

Changes. I can do without them at my age.

By the time I feel like looking again, she's with her mother and Marti, and the waterworks have started again. Marti looks awful. Of course, with me and Kati having all boys, he never had to say goodbye to a sister. Come on, though; it's a year less for you and at least you're sure of still *being* here. *And* you'll hear her voice again. They'll all be the same to me, before long.

I beckon Andras, but he's staring at her and can't see me, so I have to trust my voice: "Andras!" He turns, startled, and comes over, looking apprehensive. Don't worry, lad; I want you to listen, not talk. I hold his eyes with mine. "Be good to her."

His face clears, and he nods vigorously. "I will, I will."

"Promise."

"I promise." He kisses my hands and I pat his head in a vaguely blessing sort of way, wondering how I could do him an injury if it ever became necessary. Silly old fool.

Talking of silly old fools, I see the priest coming. It's the same one who buried my Kati and told me I had nothing to feel sad about because she was happy in heaven. Well good for her, I nearly said; how's that meant to make *me* feel any better? And how do you know she's happy, without me? I felt like sending him to find out.

Anni walks to Andras, not looking right or left, and they take hands and go, eyes locked, to stand in front of him at the table.

I nearly always nod off at this point. The service seems to go on for ever, with those damn crowns being passed to and fro all the time, and the incense makes me dizzy, even in the open air. At least the priest is inaudible this time. Everything's got its good side.

The old men – the other old men – soon get bored with him and start nattering amongst themselves. I wonder what I'm missing. Not much, I bet. It's when people have to spend ten minutes getting every futile remark across that you realise how little they say that matters. It doesn't stop you wondering, though.

I wish I couldn't hear Theo. His voice is shrill now, nothing like when he was young, and I can still hear him, asking the same pointless question, over and over, and never listening to the answer. Nobody can reach him; it's as if words have come loose from their meanings in his mind. If I thought I'd end up like that, I'd go down to the river. What's the point, eh? If you've got a deaf dog, it can still hunt and run and do whatever makes it a dog, but if it loses a couple of legs you shoot it, because it can't be a dog any more. And for a man, it's his mind; he can get by without hearing, walking, even seeing, but his mind, that's what makes him a *man* and not a mole or an insect... I don't suppose the priest would agree, though.

A glint of different light: gold, not silver. The rings on both their hands. They turn, and I see her face fixed on his, the generous mouth smiling.

Then she reaches for the other part of the veil, draws it across her face and fastens it.

5

HANNA; ANNI

Of course I wanted to come straight away, but you have to give it three days; it's traditional.

Emmi opened the door. "Oh, it's you; come in, I was expecting you." I took my shoes off – it was turning out terribly wet, for May; we were lucky to get a good day for the wedding, really – and she padded in ahead of me, to the house that always seems so quiet compared with ours. Andras was still out at work, so there was just her and the old great-aunt who lives with them. And *her*, near the inner door, so that she could slip away out of sight quickly if the visitor turned out to be a stranger. My breath caught in my chest when I saw her eyes.

Andras's mother had gone to see about coffee, so I said hello to Auntie and chatted about nothing much while I tried to speak to Anni with my eyes. She should really have gone to help Emmi make the coffee, but she couldn't take her gaze off me. I was nearly as bad. I'd forgotten, stupidly enough, that she wouldn't be wearing her everyday clothes, or rather that she'd still have the long silver-crusted coat over them; she didn't look herself in it somehow. I tried to read her eyes – I'd never realised, before, how much the corners of her mouth used to say about how she was feeling.

Auntie wasn't much use. She'd never been married, so you couldn't expect her to know what questions to ask. But generally she was a great one for gossip; it was just that this particular day, she wanted to tell me all about some other folk none of us had the least business with. When Emmi came back, though, things went all right.

"How's Marti? And everyone else in your household?"

"Fine, very well. We all miss our daughter, of course, but we're well enough in ourselves."

Anni. My name's Anni.

"Any news?"

"Not much, really. Marti's been working all hours at the yard, but you probably knew that from Andras. Nico's got into the school choir, so we hear nothing but that now. And Stevi's in trouble with his teacher again, I'm afraid. I'm sure your Andras was never such a trial at his age."

What trouble? That teacher's got a down on him. He's got a name for it; he was horrible to Edo.

Emmi laughed wryly. "Just as much, and only me to sort it out. Have a biscuit?"

"Thank you." I hesitated. "How are things here?"

"Couldn't be better. Andras seems very happy, and we all get along fine." She smiled with her eyes at Anni. I felt a bit relieved. Ever since Anni got serious with Andras, I'd tried to get to know Emmi better, but she wasn't the easiest. I'd known her as a girl, of course; very chatty and lively she was in those days. And then she married, a year or so before I did, and by the time we could speak to each other again she was already left a widow with little Andras. And she was different; everybody is, but she more than most. Much more self-contained, more inward. I sometimes felt she was talking to someone inside her head.

She was very close to Andras, naturally, not that she made much show of it but it was all there in the way they didn't have to say things. I'd been really scared she would resent whoever he brought home, but she seemed to be coping very well. I wished Anni would answer her looks more. She did try, in a watery sort of fashion, but her eyes were still on me and I could see she was hungry for my voice. Calling yourself by a different name is one thing, but it's harder to tell yourself you belong to a new family.

"Marti's old father has got over that chill we thought he was in for. I found some peaches for him in the market in town yesterday; he loves those."

"It's early for peaches."

"Yes, they came from way down south, cost a fortune, but I like to see him in humour. Ria's been very good to him, amazingly enough; stayed in and played chess with him a few times."

Ria. What does she know?

"Oh, that's nice. But he's bound to miss his other grand-daughter; she was so good at getting through to him."

Anni. My name is Anni. Use my name.

"Yes, I'm sure he does, but we're all doing our best to see he doesn't feel left out. It's hard sometimes though, when you have to repeat a thing so often..."

Change the words, then. You know he reads some shapes better than others; it's pointless saying the same things over and over.

"... but he's getting along fine, on the whole." It was so hard to strike a balance. I didn't want it to sound as if we were no different. Everyone wants to be missed. And I had to remember to mention everyone; I think I probably mentioned most of them twice, just to be sure.

What about my kitten? Who's looking after him?

I told Emmi several more things she couldn't possibly have wanted to know about our household, and she listened attentively and asked questions as if she couldn't hear enough. I was very grateful to her; she couldn't have behaved better. But then Andras was a nice lad; he didn't get that way by accident and she'd done all his bringing-up. I stayed till he came home.

(I hadn't really seen him since the wedding. Right after-wards, we'd gone up to them and Marti welcomed him into our family. Andras thanked him, and then I said: "And welcome from me too." He looked thunderstruck, and then it dawned on him and his face lit up: "Of course, I can talk to you now!" It seemed funny at the time, and I nearly laughed, till I saw her eyes.)

When he came through the door, we all perked up, just like in our house when Marti gets home. Suddenly Emmi was bustling round again, and the old auntie was twittering and laughing with him, and Anni's eyes were like a wild bird's that sees the cage door open. He went to her first and hugged her, and then sat and chatted with me while she and his mother brought the supper in. I loved being able to talk properly to him; he was a sweet-natured lad and he went out of his way to tell me how happy they were. He even asked me to stay and eat with them.

She wanted me to stay, I could see that. I wanted to stay where I could see her, too. But it wouldn't have been kind. If she and Andras could have disappeared straight to their room for a talk it might have been all right, but they'd have to get supper over first and she'd need to contain herself till then. I could see the fight she was having, to keep things in check; once or twice I was sure she'd been on the verge and had to bite it back. It takes a while before it comes natural. She was still twirling a finger, sometimes, in her veil, around where her curls would have been.

So I thanked Emmi and said goodbye to her, and to Auntie, and then turned to Andras.

"Goodbye Andras. We'll meet again soon. Wish your wife well from me." And I went home to Marti and the children.

Anni. Anni. Anni.

All right, I'm not being fair. I know why they do that, Mum told me before the wedding; his mother too. Because it's hard not to react to your name, not to speak back when you hear it. They're trying to help. It gets easier after a while, they said; it gets to be habit and you don't even think of doing it.

I don't believe it. I thought I knew all this; I'd seen friends go through it. I knew the rules; my mother and I went over them often enough. Who can you speak to, and when? Your husband, when alone with him. Your children, as soon as they're born; and then you can talk to Andras in front of others too. After the first year, your mother-in-law. In another year, your own mother. After the third year, all the women in your husband's household. After the fourth, your father and sisters. After five years, all women, and any man closely related by blood or marriage. ("Does that mean Bapa?" "Yes, Bapa, Stevi, Nico and your uncles. Brothers-in-law, if anyone'll ever have Ria; nephews some day; Andras's uncles; his father and brothers if he had any." "What about cousins?" "It's probably better to forget about cousins...") Never again any man not related by blood or marriage; never Jos's tall tales or Edo's heartaches.

It never sounded easy, of course it didn't. But it did sound possible, if only because I'd have him to talk to, and I didn't think I'd need anyone else. In those last weeks before we married, I hardly

34

did talk to anyone else; I couldn't be bothered.

The table's laid. She calls him.

"Come and sit down; supper's ready."

"I need a wash first: we've been mastering glove hides and I feel steeped in chickenshit."

I knew that already, as soon as he came through the door.

"There's hot water in the kitchen. I expect Anni can find you a towel."

They're right: it is the hardest thing to ignore. My eyes went straight to hers and my lips parted; it was only the feel of silk brushing against them that reminded me.

The kitchen isn't really "alone"; they can still see us. But Emmi's making a business of talking loudly to Auntie and clattering dishes. I help him off with his shirt and he whispers behind it: "Love you".

"I love you too." *I breathe the words into his hair; it's all silvered with little drops of rain from outside. I've been hearing the rain all day. He washes his face and arms; I dry him; the rough towel fills with whispers:* love, missed, dying, soon, you, me, talk, soon, talk, love, talk. *My words, filtered through silk; how do they sound outside? His seem so clear, I'm looking over my shoulder in case. Every word a secret. An achievement; something snatched when no-one's looking, like a kiss in the garden. We don't think of kisses; there's only a few moments and words are more precious. My stomach is knotted and my heart's thumping really hard. I can feel his body trembling under the towel. Then he goes back in, and I fold all the words up in the towel and put it away and follow him.*

Sitting at the table, watching as if from a distance: Emmi asking him about work and him answering, mentioning Dad sometimes, Jos and the lads. Auntie chirping on with some gossip she's heard; that's all wrong for a start; I could tell her...

Wanting to ask him things: to hear more about this or that. The talk going like a river, and me on the bank. The time he mentioned something that happened last year, and turned to me: "You remem..." and froze; and Emmi covered it so calmly, while he looked at me, trying to say sorry without words. At least he's got his whole face to do it with. I'm smiling reassurance behind the veil, wondering how much of it reaches my eyes.

There's nothing wrong with the food, but I can't eat much. I feel as if my throat's tightened. Andras is just picking at his food too, though he's always hungry this time of day as a rule. It's been like this since the wedding; neither of us can wait for supper to be over. Emmi never mentions it, though I've seen her glancing at what he leaves on his plate. Nothing bothers Auntie though; she just pecks busily away, talking with her mouth full, and pauses now and then to wonder where our appetite's gone.

And even when everyone's finished, there's the clearing-up: Emmi and me in the kitchen while he's in the front room and Auntie stays in there chatting to him. I reckon Emmi thinks she should be out here helping, but she goes her own sweet way, does Auntie; what she doesn't want to hear, she doesn't listen to. It means Emmi's got no-one to talk to me through, but we seem to get by, mostly. I know her routine now, and where everything goes; we generally manage to get it all done without bumping into each other too much. It's much more chaotic at our place, actually, with everyone speaking at once.

Before the wedding, when I'd come here for tea, I'd help Emmi with the clearing sometimes, when she let me, and of course we could still talk then. She'd always chat pleasantly, but even then there were silences, not unfriendly but because she was used to silence. I suppose normally she'd have been on her own in the kitchen, and I wonder sometimes if she's forgotten she still isn't. Once or twice she's turned round and given a little start, as if she hadn't expected anyone to be there. But then I hardly am.

Who could ever tell you what it's really like? Listening to people talk and not being able to join them. Spelling letters out on your fingers, making signs; anything rather than just saying thank you, or sorry, or where are the scissors, or I feel so alone... they don't teach you a sign for that one, though. You have to swallow so much; bite your lip so often. I feel as if I'm going to be sick half the time, and I swear if I was, it would be words, not food.

I'm in the middle of washing-up when I hear myself humming a tune. But I catch it early. The first day, I didn't realise what I was doing until Emmi seemed to develop a persistent cough. I'm getting a lot more control of it now. It's still embarrassing, though.

I make some unnecessary clatter with the plates, as if there were still any noise to cover, and glance across at Emmi, wondering if she's noticed. But her eyes are approving and she gives me a little nod, meaning: yes, but you're getting on top of it. And I feel a sudden rush of pride and achievement, as if I'd just sung something really well.

I'm not sure how much more of this I can stand.

6

ANDRAS

I had to notice everything; remember everything. As soon as we were alone in our room, it would be like a flood.

"What happened today? What's going on in the yard? What's new?"

I didn't make the mistake of saying "nothing much" any more, because I knew now that the smallest thing mattered to her. I tried to think back through the day, and get her veil off at the same time.

"There's a whole lot of pink flowers come out on the big tree by Tomas's... you've bitten your lip, there's blood on it here. And we got a big order for boot leather. Oh, and I heard there's a new weaving mill opening in town. Lots of jobs, someone said. Oh God, Anni, I love your hair; I miss seeing it."

"Where'd you hear about the mill?"

"In the shop. Can I undo your plaits now?"

She gave me the brush. "Was Edo there?"

"Yes, he'd just dropped a jar of coffee all over the floor and the smell was fantastic. His dad wasn't best pleased."

She grimaced. "Well, it's his own fault; he makes Edo nervous."

"He does that all right." Most of his time in the shop, Edo spent being slapped, cursed or shouted at, but on the other hand you could see the old man's point; he had a business to run, and a son who could hardly raise his eyes to customers wasn't exactly cut out for a salesman.

"Did you go round to our – my father's house today?"

"Yes, for a little while after work. They're all fine. Stevi and Nico told me another heap of jokes for you and I wrote them down this time, so I wouldn't forget. And your kitten kept playing with my bootlaces. I'll try and smuggle him over again soon, if you like." I'd brought him over once, hidden in my coat, soon after we married. Maybe my mother wouldn't have minded, but we'd never had one, because she thought they'd eat the goldfish in the garden pond. Anyway, it was kind of an adventure to smuggle him.

"How's Bapa?"

"Sitting out in the garden, enjoying the sun."

"With anybody?"

"Yeah, your mother and Ria were popping in and out to him all the time, honest. I told them what you said about changing the words, and your mother says it does make a difference. She says to tell you she'll come over tomorrow... oh, Anni, I love you; I really miss you all day."

"How about Ria? I haven't seen her in weeks."

I bent down to take my boots off. "Well, be fair, she doesn't leave school for a month or so yet. Maybe she'll come more often in summer." Anni's face looked troubled for a moment, but she nodded and accepted it.

I couldn't lie to her, but I always felt guilty if I kept anything from her, when my words were all she had. Hanna was doing her best to get Ria to come round with her, and there'd be a new excuse each time. She'd been once, early on, when I was at work, and my mother said she hardly spoke at all, or looked directly at Anni, just took sidelong glances and looked away again. I knew it wouldn't help for *me* to talk to her. I'd hoped we'd get on better after the wedding, but if anything it was worse; she didn't bother being sarky to me any more, but she was dead cold. I'd asked Hanna about it and she shook her head.

"I wish I knew, Andras, really. As far as I can see, she just can't get used to seeing Anni in a veil, and not speaking. I asked: "Why didn't you look at her?" when we came home, and she said: "Where was she?" I don't think she means to be unkind. She's just so young, and she doesn't like to think of that being her one day."

"Can't blame her really. I'm not sure I like it much myself."

She put her hand on my arm, her eyes troubled. "Why, Andras, what's wrong? I thought things were all right with you and Anni?"

"Oh they are; we love each other lots; I didn't mean to

worry you... only.... it's so hard to remember not to talk to her when anyone else is there, and I can't even see any *point* in it...."

"You always remembered not to talk to me, before you were allowed to."

"I was used to that." I sounded sulky, even to myself. She pulled my head down to her shoulder for a moment and ruffled my hair. "It gets easier. And it won't be for long. A year at most; less if a baby comes sooner."

That didn't answer the question I hadn't asked – what was the point anyway – and I still couldn't ask it; not of her, nor of my mother. And when I was talking to Anni, I didn't want to think about it at all.

I got quieter. In the yard, or on the street, I'd find myself listening to what went on, storing it up for her, rather than talking myself. I worried about her all day – was she lonely; how was she coping? Was her mother or someone else visiting, or did she have no words but what my mother and Auntie used to each other – which, it struck me for the first time, wasn't that many. On the way home, I'd feel myself tensing up, dying to see her but reminding myself, at every step, to curb my tongue when I did. As soon as I got through the door I'd run to her and hug her, and all the day's words would choke in my throat.

And then there'd be supper, and I tell you, I've never enjoyed food less, before or since. I'd always been one for rushing breakfast, working through dinnertime and making up for it in the evening, but I couldn't do it any more – I had to take bread and cheese to work with me instead. It wasn't quite so bad in the mornings, when I was about to go out anyway, but supper was really hard. She'd be sitting at my right, close enough to touch, and all I could see of her face was the eyes. In my mind I'd be picturing her long dark curly hair, and her mouth, and her little chin, and they drove me madder than if I could see them. I'd watch the veil stir ever so gently with her breath, and my throat would tighten until I couldn't swallow. I wanted the sound of her voice so badly, everyone else's was painful to me – my own, Mother's, Auntie's – and yet I had to talk to them, to get anything across to her. I'd talk to them, listen to them, thinking only of her; sometimes I lost it, just looking at her and aching, until some voice would cut across my thought like a whining saw, or a wasp on a window. My stomach felt like it had knots in it, and someone yanked on them with every mouthful I tried to eat; every trivial remark anyone made; every minute I was trapped at that table. She seemed so much further away from me than when we were engaged, and I wanted her so much more.

When we could finally close a door behind us, we went frantic. We had all night, but it seemed vital to do and say everything at once... I'd never have believed, until then, that you could kiss and talk at the same time, but it's dead easy, as is talking with your mouth full – Anni'd feed me bits of candy and fruit, which I could eat with no trouble whatever, now all the knots were loosened.

I liked to undo her plaits and brush all the hair down. It took ages, because I kept stopping to kiss and stroke it – given the choice, I'd have left the brush alone and combed it all down with my fingers. It was so electric; it crackled and hovered in the air, and every time I touched it with my lips or fingertips, there was a good chance it'd send a pulse through me. Sometimes I'd cry out, and bury my face in it to stifle the sound. But usually she was talking too much to notice.

Nothing much stopped us talking, not even love. It would turn to whispers, maybe, and soft giggles rather than laughter. She liked me to say her name a lot, and I'd whisper it over and over, like a kind of litany. *Anni, Anni, Anni...* There was never a moment, and I mean never, when I wasn't trying to gasp that name, or when she might not suddenly say something in my ear. It might sound disconcerting, and it sometimes was, but even now, when I try to imagine making love in silence, it's like a song with the words or the tune missing.

She talked in her sleep too, though nothing I could understand – I could hardly make a word out. But I'd stay awake and listen, anyway, just for the sound of her voice. And sometimes when she was asleep beside me like that, it would come over me how I was the only one she *could* talk to now; how much she depended on me, and I'd have this terrific rush of I don't know what – pride, humility, terror, all mixed up, and I'd lie awake, eyes staring at nothing, for ages.

Sometimes at the yard I'd have a bout of yawning, and the lads would tease me about not getting enough sleep – not as much as they would have done usually, though, because it was a bit awkward around Marti, being her dad. Once though, when I was working with him on something and being a bit slow, he said quietly: "What's the matter; is she keeping you awake talking all night?"

"Oh God, no; I'm sorry, Marti, I know I've been a bit dopey lately. I'll try to sort myself out, honest. And it isn't Anni; I've been lying awake at night, but it isn't her fault. I just worry about her a lot."

His face creased into a brief grin and he said: "Good. But mind what you're doing here." Marti didn't have much patience with bad work, and I knew he meant the warning. But he loved Anni too.

"By the way," he said after a while, just a bit too casually, "Edo asked for another chance in the yard, and I said all right."

"Why?"

"Wants to get away from the shop, I suppose."

"No, I mean why say yes? He didn't even turn up last time."

"Maybe he will now. I think he's desperate to get away from his old man."

"Yes, but... you know what scared him off last time; he couldn't face all that first-day stuff with the lads. The ritual; the welcoming ceremony, whatever you like to call it. And I can't believe he will now."

"We had a word about it."

"Did you promise him it wouldn't happen?"

"No. If I did that, the lads would probably make sure it did anyway, or something worse. Or they'd resent him for not having gone through it, and he'd never be one of them. I told him it wouldn't be as bad as he thought."

I didn't say anything, and we worked on for a bit.

"I thought," he said, even more casually, "it might not be so bad for him if we could keep lads like Simo out of it .... the ones who enjoy it for all the wrong reasons."

"Well, maybe... who then?"

"Jos, Lucian, Ivo and you", he said, without a moment's hesitation, and I cursed myself for walking into it.

"Oh no, Marti, leave me out; you know I hate all that. Please."

"It has to be you; you're the only one he'll definitely trust."

"Edo doesn't trust *anybody*. Look, when we were all in school, right, in the gym, we'd have to vault the big horse. In pairs; one vaults and the other stands by the mat to steady him? Well, fair enough, there were some lads none of us trusted. Simo, who was a singular bastard even then. Benni.... They'd end up with each other, so they both knew what to expect. But Edo was scared stiff even with boys like me and Jos who'd never picked on him. If we didn't drop him on purpose, he figured we would by accident, and half the time he was right, because just looking at him all white-faced made us so nervous we couldn't have held on to fly paper. He'd veer aside at the horse, or if he did jump, he'd try to land it on his own; he'd rather break an ankle than trust anyone else. He went rigid in your grip; just wouldn't let himself go with it."

He let me finish babbling, and said calmly: "He trusted Anni, and you're Anni's man. We'll see how it goes".

I was dead sure how it was going to go; it was going to be a disaster, but I knew better than to carry on telling him what he didn't want to hear. I just said: "Yes, boss", and he gave me a sharp look and then decided to let it be.

When I was brushing Anni's hair that night, she said: "You've gone a bit quiet; is anything on your mind?"

"No, nothing... well, your dad was saying he might give Edo another go in the yard."

"So what's wrong with that?"

"Just not sure it'll work out, that's all. Edo isn't too good with people."

"He'll be all right if they don't tease him or scare him. He always was with me."

"Oh yes? Should I be jealous?" And that sort of changed the

subject, and whatever we said next was mixed up with kisses and her hair. And I was happy, if a little guilty that I hadn't told her everything, again.

7

Hanna; Anni

I met Emmi in the shop. She used to go earlier in the morning than me, but these days she seems to be there later, or maybe I'm getting earlier. She nodded and said hello, while I tried to adjust my eyes to the half-dark. It always seemed worse in summer; because Ossi kept the blinds down to stop the sun fading his dry goods, and you'd step out of the sun into this poky gloom.

"How are the young couple?"

She raised an eyebrow. "I should think you see as much of Andras as I do, these days. The lass is fine. It's nice to have some company about the place when he's gone. We spend a lot of time out in the garden, these warm days; she was helping me root some cuttings yesterday."

"Good grief! She never did a thing in the garden, when she was at home."

Emmi shrugged. "Nor did I, until it was the only place I could go outside the house."

Edo was behind the counter, being busy with something, but I knew he was listening to every word. I dropped my voice a bit.

"Any sign of her...?"

"It's early days for that."

"Oh I know, I know. I should take my own advice; I keep telling Andras it won't be long till they can talk to each other anywhere they like again. But it *seems* long, whatever anyone says. I wouldn't have thought a couple of months could go so slowly, and there's the rest of the year yet."

"At least it *is* only a year now. Back when I was married, my in-laws were still clinging on to the old ways; you could speak when you had the first child and not before. I didn't speak to my mother-in-law, or at all outside our room, for eighteen months."

"Never! I thought that went out in our mothers' day?"

"It lasted longer than that. His folk were old-fashioned, yes, but it was still going on when we were children. Didn't you ever hear about Mina?"

"Mina... no... wait, yes. She died of that fever that came through, years back... I was only about seven and my little brother died of it too, so I didn't notice much else, but I remember someone saying that. They called her some cruel name."

"Mad Mina, yes. It wasn't the fever either, though the family put that about. She'd been married six years and no child; never carried one past a few months. After three years, they said she could talk to her mother-in-law and mother, because they could see she was getting a bit peculiar. But she wouldn't."

"Why ever not?"

Emmi shrugged and spread her hands. "Maybe she felt she had to do one thing right. I didn't know much about her either, at that age, but I must have listened behind more doors than you did, because I heard someone tell my mother she did away with herself. I didn't understand what it meant, then, and I couldn't very well ask her and admit how I'd heard it... I suppose that's why it stayed in my mind."

I couldn't speak. My mind was full of poor Mina, and Anni. I picked up a little bottle of orange-flower oil, and then remembered she was the only one in the house who used it.... I put it down and looked for sweets for Ria and the lads instead.

Emmi was signing to Edo how much flour she wanted him to weigh out; it didn't look much for four, and I wondered if Anni was off her food. Edo was doing all right, until he saw his father come in, and then straight away he spilt some. His father slapped him around the ear.

"Do you want to bankrupt me, you useless little sod?"

I flinched, as if it were me he'd hit. I hated hearing him talk to his own child like that. The lad didn't flinch, nor show any expression, but his fingers were suddenly all thumbs; he couldn't pick a thing up without looking as if he'd drop it. I smiled at him with my eyes, but he looked suspicious, as if I might be mocking him. I wished so much that I could use my voice to comfort him.

46

As we left, we could still hear him being shouted at. "Oh, and you can forget that bloody yard until your brother gets out of school. I need someone in here, even if it's only you."

Emmi let out a deep breath. "What a happy family. Sometimes I wish I could tell that old goat he makes matters worse every time he opens his mouth."

"It'd probably just lead to an argument. If you ask me, that's one advantage we have, being able to avoid arguing with folk like that. After my first year, when my mother-in-law and I could talk again, there were an awful lot of times I wished we couldn't."

Emmi laughed. "She never minded a good scrap, old Kati; I remember. We had a few differences, while I was seeing her precious son. But she didn't bear any grudges, as I recall; we'd say all sorts of things neither of us regretted, and then next day she'd have forgotten all about it."

"Oh, I daresay she expected me to do that, but I couldn't. I'd remember every word that was said, hers and mine, and wish they hadn't been. It's a lot easier to bite things back, than *get* them back once they're said."

"Easier, maybe." Emmi paused outside her door. "Is Andras getting impatient with things, then?"

"Well, he doesn't see the point of it. Our Ria's like that too... I sometimes think it won't last much longer, Emmi. They say it doesn't happen in the city any more. And in some of the towns it's maybe a month, or three days, just a sort of token."

"Mm. I've heard that. Come in for a while?"

The house looked brighter somehow – there were a lot of flowers in jugs for one thing. Auntie was doing some sort of intricate lace work. She was very good at it, for what it was worth. I never saw her knitting socks, or hemming shirts, or anything else useful. She painted birds' eggs too, and stuck things on them to make patterns. She gave most of them away as ornaments; most folks had one or two about the place, though in our house they never lasted long, what with boys and cats. It was just a pastime, really.

There was no sign of Anni. Emmi cocked an ear up the stairwell.

"She goes up to their room for a quiet sing sometimes. Can't hear her now, though."

"Emmi, if it's changed in the town; if it changes here... what was it ever for?"

She raised an eyebrow, thinking. "It wouldn't have lasted so long, unless it... I can hear her coming in from the garden."

And she ran in, with an armful of flowers, and stopped dead, smiling, when she saw me. There was no hint of the veil stirring around her mouth, though. On her forehead and around her eyes, she'd caught the sun a bit, and I thought: when she takes that veil off she'll have a stripe right across her face, just as I always do in summer. And I felt a pang, and couldn't think why.

She had some pollen on her eyelashes. I brushed it off. Emmi looked on, smiling, and said to Auntie: "There's another jug in the kitchen, isn't there?" Auntie plainly didn't have a clue, but Anni disappeared with the flowers and Emmi laughed.

"I'm lucky, these days, if I can find a jug to do any cooking with; she's got them all full. I'll make some coffee, if she hasn't had the kettle." I watched her follow Anni out, and thought: it's really good that they get on so well. I should feel happy about it.

"Ooh, listen to this." That was Auntie's chirrup; if sparrows could talk they'd sound just like that. She'd lost interest in the lace and was reading a newspaper from the town. She read me the article, some poor girl murdered, with all the horrible details.

"Isn't that awful? You can't believe anyone would want to do that."

No, nor read about it, I thought, but didn't say. I just agreed with her and hoped she wouldn't read me any more. But she'd already dropped it, wanting to know all the gossip from our place. She couldn't know enough about her neighbours, Auntie, and yet I never got the impression she *cared* much about them; any more than for this girl in the town she didn't know. Still, Anni was back, so I was happy to talk about what mattered to her.

"Everyone's well, thank you; in fact I'm dreading next week when school's out. I just hope the fine weather keeps up, or the house will be like a bear-garden. It's not so bad when they can spend all day out of doors."

"You should bring them all round one day," said Emmi, "and the old man, too. He seemed to enjoy himself, last time he came with you."

"Oh he did; in fact this is the only place I can *get* him to go out to. He loves seeing... everyone here. And it's good for him; he's getting very inward. Half the time, when we try to get through to him, involve him in what's going on, he just nods or says yes or no, as if it's got nothing to do with him."

It has got nothing to do with him. He sat there on the edge of things; every so often someone remembered him and said something, but it wasn't part of the conversation; that would have gone on just the same if he hadn't been there. It didn't need him; it didn't miss him, any more than a river misses a fish. He looked at me all the time, because my eyes said the same thing his were saying. I'm here. I'm still here: stop and need me; will you even miss me when I'm gone?.

Auntie was rummaging in Emmi's basket. She straightened up and asked: "Didn't you get the beads?"

Emmi grimaced. "No, I forgot, with that business about the flour. Poor Edo, eh? What was all that about the yard – is he trying to get away again?"

"Yes, there was some talk of it, Marti said – or maybe Andras told me, I can't remember. It doesn't look as if he will, though, does it?"

"Pity. It'd be good for him to work with lots of people; bring him out of his shell a bit. He's scared of his own shadow, that one."

His father's shadow, maybe. And his teacher's. And Simo's and Benni's and everyone else's who laughed at him and gave him a hard time for being different. He's on the edge of things too, only he was born there. I wonder if you can go from the edge to the centre? You can go the other way all right. It's like a merry-go-round that pushes you out from the middle as it spins; if you didn't cling on you could fly off altogether. When Bapa was here, I looked at him

49

and thought: he's letting go; he can't grip much longer....

"He used to be all right when he came round to our place; quiet, yes, and he was scared of Ria, but then again who isn't? He could talk to Anni and the boys all right."

I'd used her name deliberately, because she seemed so distant, so wrapped up in her thoughts; I wondered if she was listening at all. She put me in mind of the old man at home, and then I thought of poor Mina... Everyone is different, when they come out of it. There was maybe the slightest little stir of the head, when she heard the name, but nothing more.

Suddenly I was scared she'd end up in a place where I couldn't reach her. I talked on and on about Marti, Ria and the boys, the cats and dogs, anything that I thought might fix her attention, as if they were lines I could hold her by. I thought of when Stevi was little, and Marti warned him to hold on with both hands to the string of his kite, or it'd get away from him. And he pointed into the sky, and Stevi looked up and saw all the clouds, and said: "Kites"....

When it was time to go, I hugged her for ages, and she seemed as warm as ever, not changed to me. But would I be able to tell? How slowly would a thing like that happen; would the string snap all at once or just part one strand at a time, so that you hardly felt her floating off?

I didn't say anything to Emmi, when she saw me out at the door, but I suppose I must have looked worried.

"She's in a daydream, that's all; you wouldn't think anything of it, if she could speak."

I shook my head.

"Stay till Andras gets in, then, and watch her come to life. I'm sure he'd like to see you, anyway"

"I'd better get the shopping home."

"Whatever." She smiled that odd smile that always seems to raise one of her eyebrows; I used to think it was sarcastic, until I got to know her. "Some things start to matter more to them, some less. Doesn't do to hold too tight; at least so I'm always telling myself."

8

ANNI; ANDRAS

It's been ten days now. But I was late last month too; not this late though... I'm not going to get my hopes up: I'm not. I got so excited last time when it was a week, I nearly told Andras.

Mum said you had to miss twice, to be sure. Or was it three times? And it's been haywire since I left home anyway.

I can't remember half of what she told me. We never really talked about anything like that until I was on the verge of getting married, and then I wasn't listening...

This is the worst time of day. It's too soon to start the supper; we've done all the work there was about the house, and there's nothing to do but sit around and sew, or knit – or talk, except for me.

I brought the washing in from the garden, a while ago, and didn't notice there was a tangle of grass and stuff stuck to my shoe when I came in. It got all over the carpet and Emmi wasn't best pleased, to judge by her face when she pointed to the doormat. I'm always forgetting it's there; in our place – my old place – the dogs were in and out all the time, and the boys were nearly as bad, so no-one noticed.

Auntie's playing with her birds' eggs, decorating one with tiny silver beads. It must need very steady hands, but it doesn't stop her chatting to Emmi all the time. Emmi's knitting. She hardly ever needs to look at it; she can read or talk to someone and all the while it's in her lap, with her fingers flying through it. Mum can do that too, but if I try it, I drop stitches. Used to drop stitches.

"The lads from next door brought me these, from the nests in the river bank. It's an ill wind; usually all they think about is swimming, but the river's so low, they were at a loose end."

"Thought kingfisher eggs were white."

"They are: I painted it. This must be the hottest summer we've had for years."

"Can't remember the river being too low to swim in before, that's a fact."

"Oh, it has been; don't you recall that drought – what; more than twenty years back now? Even the pool below the weir was dry that year."

"Oh yes, *that* year... I was carrying Andras all through the hottest of it."

It's just idle chat; it means nothing. Except what they share and I don't. Knowing how the river looks this month. Memories. What someone said in the shop. They've got so much in common; so much I'm outside of.

I could escape to the garden. But it's really hot; it makes my head ache after a while. It'll be cooler in the evening, when Andras is home. Maybe we can sit out there tonight, instead of upstairs.

Anyway, if I went out there now it might look as if I was sulking. I'm not, honestly, but I feel really choked up. I don't think Emmi's cross with me any more, but it isn't that. I can't stop thinking of our house, and how different it is here. Everything here has a place to be in, and it looks wrong if it's anywhere else. Emmi and Auntie seem to be just naturally tidy like that – Andras isn't; he just drops things anywhere, but then Emmi picks them straight up again. I'm thinking about dog footprints and schoolbooks left around the floor and cats knocking things off the mantelpiece and wishing I was there. I feel as if I'm the only thing here without a place to be in.

Maybe someone will call. No, that's worse; it just makes a bigger circle to be on the outside of. Unless it's Bapa, and he wouldn't come out in this heat. I haven't seen him in weeks.

Why would anyone want to paint a kingfisher's egg? She's done it a pretty colour, sort of rose-pink and it goes well with the silver, but it would have been just as good as it was.

Maybe I could go to our room and have a sing. They won't hear me; I do it really quietly. But it's so stuffy up there in this heat. And it worries me a bit if I go off on my own; it makes me feel like Edo. I feel if I don't stay among them, cling on to the edge of the circle, I might spin off altogether.

I seem to have been mending this shirt for ages – I never was any good at sewing. My head hurts, with that or the heat, and I'd like to stop, but then I wouldn't have an excuse to keep looking down. And I need to, because my eyes keep filling up.

Please don't stay late at the yard tonight.

I'd had a lousy day at work. I'm not giving it for an excuse, but it's true. There was some bug going round and a lot of the lads were down with it. It wasn't just the lads either; the yard dogs were off their food, so instead of chewing the flesh off the raw hides they just lay about and let it stink.... They say you get used to the smells in a tannery and of course you do, mostly, or you couldn't live, but rotting meat at the height of summer still gets through to most folk. I felt vaguely sick all day and couldn't eat when it came to the break. And then in the afternoon I was grinding bark.

We all do it from time to time, even Marti if everyone else is busy, because it's the one thing you can't do without. There's no tannin without bark, and it needs a hell of a lot of the stuff at that, so without a constant supply everything comes to a stop. But there's nearly always some kid you can put on the job, and let's face it, we do, if we can, because everyone hates doing it.

I was in that bloody bark shed for ages, with the dust from the mill flying all around. Or carrying the ground stuff to the pits, and if anything it was worse outside, with the air so dry and nothing to damp it down. My throat felt like someone had rasped the inside of it, and I swear I could feel the dust down in my lungs.

Shifting hides seemed easy, after that, but it didn't help my mood. Jos glanced at my hair, stiff with dust, and joked: "Marriage is aging you, mate; you're grey already."

"Working with a bunch of schoolboy idiots, more like."

"Hey, what's bitten you?"

"Nothing. I didn't mean it. It's the dust in my throat, that's all; it makes me ratty."

"Yeah? What was it yesterday, then, and the day before that?"

I didn't say anything, and we finished off in silence, which suited me all right just then. I was beginning to feel I'd had enough of words.

When we knocked off, Jos turned to me at the yard gate.

"Come down the Eagle tonight with us, after you've eaten."

"Ah... thanks, but I'd better not."

"Why? You need to get out and relax, mate; spend some time with your friends. You've been hellish edgy lately. Anni wouldn't mind by now, would she?"

"No, of course not. I just don't feel like it."

"Suit yourself."

Marti had just come out of his office and caught the end of what we'd said. He watched Jos walk off whistling, then turned to me.

"Have you two had a row?"

"No, he was just trying to get me to go down the pub with him later, that's all."

"Maybe you should."

"I don't feel like it." As soon as Jos had mentioned it, I knew I really wanted to; there was nothing I felt like more. And every time I thought it, I felt guiltier, because it wasn't that I wanted to spend time with the lads, particularly. It was more to do with what I didn't want. I wanted not to have to spend hours talking about the day I'd had, and the day she'd had, and reassuring her that people hadn't forgotten she was there; that we'd surely start a baby soon; that Bapa was all right – he hadn't been out for a while, and she didn't trust her family not to lie to her about it. But I was the truth-teller, the one who told her everything and listened to everything, and it was killing me. I despised myself for even thinking that, knowing I couldn't begin to imagine how much worse it must be for her. But I knew I did think it.

It tied me up in knots, and I hardly spoke on the way home, but Marti knew I had the bark dust in my throat so he didn't make anything of it. When we parted, though, he said again: "Maybe you should go and spend time with the lads."

I denied again that I wanted to, and wondered what he'd think of me if he knew how I really felt. The mere thought made me go hot with embarrassment. I hated getting on the wrong side of him at work, because he didn't get mad like most folks do – you know: flare up, say something you'll regret, and then calm down. He was a cold angry man; it took him ages to get angry, but when he did he never lost control; he said exactly what he meant to, and it could really hurt. And that was work: I didn't dare even guess what he'd be like when his family was involved.

As soon as I was through the door, Anni ran to me and hugged me. I hugged her too, briefly, but my throat couldn't wait.

"Get me some water, Mum, for God's sake." Anni looked ready to rush off and do it, but my mother was in the kitchen already, so she brought it through. I drank and drank, and it felt good at the time, but the relief didn't seem to last; in a few moments it'd be as bad as ever, and I'd have to go back to the water-jug. It hurt to swallow food too, which was a pest, seeing I was dead hungry.

Auntie was as chatty as ever – you'd have thought, after all this time, she'd realise what the dust did, but she never seemed to – and I could feel my mood getting worse every time I had to answer a question. Anni reached out and squeezed my hand, under the table. I tried to smile at her, but it was in my mind that her eyes didn't look very happy, as if she'd had a bad day, and I thought: I'm going to have to listen to it all later.

After supper we went up to our room as usual and I closed the door behind us. It felt cramped and stuffy; it would have been nice to leave the door open, but then of course we couldn't have talked.

"You must have been in the bark shed for ages, poor thing."

"Felt like it."

"We could sit out in the garden. It'd be cooler for you there, and we could still talk."

"In a while, maybe. I need a rest first."

"Auntie said the river's dried up."

"In places. The weir's still deep enough."

I was hardly giving anything back, and I could sense that she was puzzled and concerned. She'd seen Marti come home with a throatful of bark dust often enough; me too, and she knew it should have eased a bit by now. I knew that too. Something was making words come hard, but it wasn't the dust.

"What's the matter?"

"Oh God, Anni, don't make me talk, all right; just leave it."

She looked at me but didn't say anything, just went and sat by the window, staring out at the street.

"I'm sorry. Work was hell today. Christ, it's hot in here. This place is like a prison."

"You don't have to stay in it."

"What's that supposed to mean?"

"Nothing."

I didn't reply, and there was silence for a while, until she said: "Do you want to go down and talk to the others?"

"Not particularly."

"I don't mind."

"I said no."

"Well you might as well, if you're going to be like this."

"Like what? Like flaming what?"

"Like you'd rather be anywhere else."

"Maybe you'd rather I went out altogether?"

Her eyes rested on my face, as if they were trying to read it.

"If that's what you want to do, you don't need to start a row for an excuse."

I was angry with her – God knows what for, unless it was for seeing through me too easily – and I clung to the anger because without it, I'd have been feeling something harder to live with. I grabbed my jacket from the nail she'd hung it on.

"Where are you going?"

"Don't know. For a walk. Down to the river, maybe."

Her eyes looked anguished. Some remains of decency in me suggested that saying: "I'm going for a walk" to someone who couldn't leave the house wasn't the kindest thing you could do. But instead of thinking better of it, I got out all the faster.

Down to the river. No, he didn't mean it like that. He's just gone for a walk. Anyway it's dry... not by the weir; there's still the deep pool. This is daft. He's gone for a walk. A walk. He'll be back soon.

I suppose I knew from the start where I was going. I did walk around for a bit; maybe I wanted to persuade myself I just fetched up in the Eagle by accident. Jos and some of the others were there.

"Hey, mate, glad you changed your mind! Anni let you out, then?"

"Yeah, no bother." I felt like Judas. No: like Peter.

"Have a beer." I did, and a few more. I don't know if Peter felt better after a couple of beers, but it worked for me. I felt less tense than I had for ages. Free, let out, one of the lads again. I was laughing and chatting like I hadn't a care in the world. Except every so often there'd be this ache when I thought about her, and a worse one when I thought about me, and then I'd need another beer to make it go away.

9

ANDRAS

I woke up next morning with a dry throat and my head thumping. I hadn't drunk all that much, but I was well out of the habit of it too, so it really got to me. Anni watched me knock back about half a jug of water, not saying anything. Everyone had been asleep when I got home, and if my barging round the room had woken her, she hadn't let on.

I suppose I was on edge for her to say something like: *you were late home,* or *no wonder you don't feel too good,* and maybe I'd have snapped back with *so what,* or *can't I go out once in a while?* But she said nothing, and it made me feel more edgy than ever.

She got dressed as usual, but she started plaiting her hair herself, instead of asking me to help as I always did, and I didn't offer. I just felt hurt about it, and at the back of hurt was guilt, and a resentment about feeling guilty that was close to anger.

When I opened our door to go down, she stayed sitting at the window.

"Aren't you coming down for breakfast?"

"I'm not hungry. Say sorry to Emmi for me and tell her I'll come down and help in a little while. I don't feel too well."

She didn't look well either; she looked a bit washed-out. I felt guilty again, and then angry: *surely going down the pub doesn't cause all this,* and hurt, because I reckoned "in a little while" meant "when you've left for work". And I said: "Right; fine", which must have been just about the opposite of anything I wanted to say, and went down.

My mother looked concerned when I gave her the message, and went up to see her. She wasn't very communicative when she came back, and I took it she was siding with Anni against the village drunk. I picked at some food and told Auntie some of the more repeatable gossip I'd heard down the pub. *She* didn't seem to disapprove of me, anyway.

Mother gave me the bread and cheese she'd packed me for the yard, and I started for the door.

"Aren't you going to say goodbye to her?"

"I expect she wants to rest, if she isn't well."

My mother gave me a long look, and said drily: "Feeling sorry for yourself must be more fun than I thought." Whatever I'd said next, I would have regretted, so I walked out of the door, feeling furious with everyone in the place, including the goldfish. Marti was just coming along the street, and I fell in beside him.

But I couldn't stop myself looking up at our window, and she was there, looking smaller somehow and her eyes sad, and her face white, what I could see of it for the damn veil. And I nearly called out to her to make it up, before I remembered I mustn't.

I should have gone back, right then. But there was my mother, and Auntie, and while I could face saying sorry to *her*, something in me wasn't ready to admit in front of them that I'd been wrong, by walking back in the house. I told myself it'd do in the evening.

Marti had looked up at the window too, and waved to her. She waved back; she even managed a smile. Her pride was a lot more use than mine. It didn't fool him, though.

"Anything wrong?" he asked, as we fell into step again.

"No. Everything's fine." Even as the words left my mouth, I knew it was the stupidest thing I could have said; everything plainly wasn't fine, and he was bound to be worried. I could have told him all about it; part of me wanted to, but it just felt too hard to put into words. I even tried to work up a bit of indignation in my mind: I'd only done just what he'd suggested, after all.... I walked on, saying nothing, and he was unusually silent too.

Once we were at work, Marti went about his business as normal, while I carried on trying to earn a diploma in stupidity. I might as well not have been there, I was so churned up inside my head. That was how it happened.

I'd had some glove leathers in the mastering pit, softening up in that awful soup of shit and hot water – I swear, if gentlefolk knew how leather gloves were made, they'd all be knitting wool ones – and then I'd left them to get on with it. I was on the roller with Ivo in the currying shed, but I kept thinking about Anni and last night and that morning, and my mind just wasn't on the job. I couldn't stop going over all I'd said, and why it was nothing like what I'd wanted to say. And what she hadn't said, and what it meant that she hadn't said it... And in the end I forgot the damn hides altogether, until about mid-day when I saw Jos coming toward me with what looked like a bunch of leather hankies.

"Oh Christ!"

The one thing you can't do is leave hides in that stuff too long, or it reduces them like you'd never believe. They were beautiful quality, the best we had, and they were ruined.

Jos put a hand on my shoulder.

"He knows, mate. I'm sorry. Me and Luc were stacking, and he walks by and says: who's had hides in the master? And we tell him, not thinking any harm, and he says: well go and get them out and tell him I want him. I'm sorry."

"Oh Christ. Oh Christ."

"Come on, mate, it could be worse. At least he isn't like some bosses; he won't hit you. But he's gone real quiet and cold, so I wouldn't make him any madder. Best come and get it over."

He was standing by his little site office near the main gate, with his back to me. Some of the lads looked up and crossed fingers for me as we passed, but they didn't dare stop work altogether.

Jos said: "He's here, boss." Marti didn't turn, just pointed to a spot in front of him, so I went and stood there.

He was as angry as I'd ever seen him. I knew how long it took him to get that cold, and I knew it wasn't about some ruined hides ten minutes back. He'd been working up to this all morning.

I felt my guts clench. Like Jos said, Marti had never hit a workman in his life, but it occurred to me that if he was ever going to start, it might be now. And if he did, it wouldn't be because he'd lost control; he'd be dead calm.... Somehow that made it scarier. He stood over me, looking down, and I couldn't read his face.

"I'm sorry, boss. For everything."

He held my eyes with his for what felt like weeks.

"If you need fewer distractions from work, I can arrange it."

He turned, and called: "Jos!"

"Yes, boss?"

"Him", he jerked a thumb back over his shoulder at me, "nobody speaks to him, he speaks to nobody. Until I say different. Tell Leo in the beam house, and anyone else out of earshot."

"Yes, boss."

"Get back to work, the rest of you."

Ivo'd followed me and Jos over – I hadn't even noticed. He gave me a rueful grin and jerked his head towards the roller.

We walked back and finished there. Then we knocked off to eat. Jos and some of the others came over and they talked, a bit subdued at first, as if they were embarrassed in front of me. But pretty soon they loosened up and chatted away as if I wasn't there. It felt weird. I was glad when we went back to work, though not for long.

All afternoon, whatever I was doing, I had to keep it in mind. Not ask anyone to pass anything. Not react when Simo kept saying my name or making sarky remarks. Not thank anyone in words. Not cap jokes nor join in crosstalk. Words kept nearly bubbling over; I'd choke them down; it was like fighting back tears or stopping yourself being sick. I took to biting down hard on my bottom lip all the time to try to remind myself. Once, helping to shift hides, I dropped the long-handled tongs and said "sorry", before I thought. It fell on total silence and I didn't know where to look. Nor did the lads, and I nearly said sorry again for embarrassing them. They were sympathetic, most of them, and I got a lot of kind looks through the day, but they wouldn't have dared go against the boss in that mood, and I wouldn't have wanted them to. I knew well enough what he was doing.

It did get a bit easier to remember not to speak, after a while, but that was because I started to feel I was behind glass, that everything was happening at a great distance, instead of all around me, and I was standing watching it, not part of it any more. It was like it could all go on without me, and never notice. I've never felt so alone, and I know it sounds daft, but there were moments I was close to panic. I wouldn't have believed how much a passing smile or a gesture from someone could mean, after just a few hours of it. It was like proof I still existed. There was one time; the sweat was pouring off me, getting my eyes all salty, and I had both hands full so I couldn't do a thing about it, and I couldn't ask anyone else to. Jos reached over and dried my forehead. It was an everyday sort of thing; anyone would do it for anyone and often enough you wouldn't need to ask, but the way I was placed, it meant so much more that someone bothered; it could make all the difference.

When we knocked off, I couldn't get away fast enough. But I hadn't got far when Marti caught me up. We walked side by side, as usual, but not speaking – I wasn't sure whether the ban ended at the yard gate and I thought I'd better wait for him to say something first. He didn't; we got right back to the village without either of us saying a word.

Halfway along the street he heaved a huge sigh and rested his arm on my shoulder. I turned to him and made to speak, but he put his hand over my mouth and shook his head.

I'd thought it was all over, and I had a moment of blind panic – how long was this going to last? Days? Weeks? And almost at once, I thought of her, and how many days and weeks had it been since May the seventeenth, and I felt sick with shame. I buried my face in my hands, and right then, all I wanted in the world was for him to know that I wasn't crying about what was happening to me, but about what had been happening to her. And I couldn't think how, not without words. I looked up and saw our house, a little way along, and I pointed to the window of our room up top, and then to my heart, and.... how the hell do you say "sorry" without words? I stretched my hands out to the window, howled with frustration inside, and looked hopelessly at him.

But maybe something got through after all, because he

smiled slightly, turned me back toward my door and gave me a gentle push in the direction of it. Well, it was meant to be gentle, I think, but he was built like a bear, so I was lucky to keep my footing.

I ran to my door and barged in, straight past Auntie, open-mouthed in her chair, and my mother was standing at the kitchen door looking a bit surprised, and I ran past her too, muttering "sorry, sorry", and into the kitchen.

And she was there, at the cupboard, just reaching up for some plates, and I caught her hands and kissed them. She looked pale and tired, but her eyes lit up and she smiled.

I turned to ask my mother to leave us alone in the kitchen, but she was already closing the door behind her. I swear sometimes I think she's a witch; she's always been able to read my mind or my face or something.

But me, I'm just ordinarily thick, and it's hard enough with words. I turned back to Anni, seeing how her eyes sparkled, and how red the rims were, and I said the only word I seemed to have been saying or wanting to say all day. Only at last I was saying it in the right place.

10

ANNI; ANDRAS

I didn't feel right at all when I woke, and my first thought was: oh God, it can't come after all, not after ten weeks.... But it hadn't. And it wasn't quite that feeling anyway, not that dragging ache. More like the heat had got to me, maybe; but the worst of that was over, too.

Helping Emmi get breakfast ready was murder; just the sight of food made me feel queasy. I tried to eat, though, hoping it'd settle my stomach, but I could only nibble at it. Andras looked worried, so I ate a bit more, but I gave most of it to him in the end.

After he left, Auntie wandered out to the garden while Emmi and I started to put the plates together. But almost at once I felt really awful. I tried to get to the garden, but I'd only gone a few steps when I was sick all over the carpet.

I'd never felt so embarrassed. It would have been bad enough even in our house, but here.... I lowered my eyes to the floor for a few moments and raised them again; it's just as well "sorry" is so easy to sign. But Emmi shook her head, and stopped me when I went to get a cloth.

She made me sit down, while she cleaned up the mess. Then she came back to the table and moved her hand in front of my stomach, eyebrows raised. I nodded.

Her eyes widened and lit up; I could hear her intake of breath and see the veil stir over her mouth; for a moment I thought she'd speak. But she asked the question with her eyes after all, and her hand held up like a witness: is it certain? I shrugged, and held up both hands, fingers crossed. I think so.

She spread three fingers, one by one, and asked with her eyes again. I counted off two. She gestured at the damp patch of carpet, and I held up one. She smiled all over her face – yes, you can tell, – and patted my shoulder briefly. Then she gestured me to stay where I was, and ran off upstairs.

She came back with an armful of baby clothes. They must have been Andras's and she'd kept them all this time, even after her husband died and she knew there wouldn't be any more.... well, I suppose a widow could remarry, but Emmi wouldn't have considered it. I just knew. She laid them down, little cotton shirts, woolly hats, jackets and shawls, his lace christening robe. They all smelt of lavender, and as she held each one up, the grey seeds shook out of them. She mimed how she'd laid them by in layers of paper, with the lavender to keep them fresh.

We swept the breakfast things to one end of the table and spread them out in the space we'd made. They were so tiny. It was years since Nico'd been a baby, and I was only about six when he was born; I could hardly remember. I must have seen plenty of babies since, but it seemed as if I could never have really taken notice of them. I couldn't believe they were as small as this. I pointed to the littlest shirt and held my hands close together, and she nodded and laughed softly. She picked up a woolly hat and mimicked Andras trying to fit it on his head now, and I shook with laughter and had to press my hands over my mouth. We were both getting fairly silly, when we heard Auntie on her way in from the garden.

I looked up at Emmi in a bit of a panic – Auntie was the sort to run out and gossip it all over the place, before I was even sure. Emmi just dropped a cloth over the things, her normal calm self in an instant. Auntie gave the table a surprised glance, but she was looking at the other end.

"My, you two are slow today. I thought you'd have things cleared by now."

Emmi and I looked at each other: two girls with a secret, we know something you don't, just like in school. Auntie pottered about as usual, rearranging some flowers that were perfectly all right in the first place, while Emmi picked up the cloth-wrapped bundle and put it beside her chair, with her knitting. She gave me a look that said "as soon as she's gone", and we started taking the plates through to the kitchen.

When we were safely in there, I gestured back at Auntie and put my finger to my lips. Emmi just gave me an incredulous glance, as if to say: did you even suppose I'd think of it? Then she winked at me. And I knew something, suddenly, that I'd never known before, and yet as soon as I thought it, I could see it had always been so:

Emmi couldn't be bothered with Auntie at all. They'd lived in the same house all these years, able to talk, too, but they might have been a sheep and a horse in the same field, for all they had in common. It had never been Emmi and Auntie; never would be. It might be Emmi and me, though.

Auntie wandered out to the shop later; she never actually did much shopping, but she went for the gossip. We knew she'd be gone ages, and we made a dive for the bundle again. I still felt worried, though, in case it was all a mistake. I made the "is it certain?" sign to Emmi and she nodded. She seemed sure enough. I felt helpless; I didn't know anything about what was happening to me, or what was going to happen next. I threw my hands out, wishing I could say it.

Emmi thought a moment, then started spelling on her fingers, counting off the letters one by one. That works all right for short messages, like names. She spelt out "Hanna" and gestured at the door, eyebrows raised.

It was tempting. If she fetched Mum, they could talk to me through each other. And I wanted to tell her – I mean, I wanted her to know. But then my folks would all know before he did, and it didn't seem right. It took ages, but finally I shook my head and spelt out: "Andras first". She nodded, as if she'd known what I would say.

It was hours before he'd be back, of course, and I thought they'd seem endless, but it was amazing how they filled up. We looked through the clothes for any that needed mending or buttons sewing on, and sorted that out. Then we packed them all in paper again, except Emmi kept out one of the little cotton shirts and a woolly jacket, signing that we'd need more of them. We took the rest upstairs and put them in the big chest in our bedroom, mine and Andras's, that is. I suppose she must have kept them in her room till then, and I wondered how it felt for her, things moving on like this.

Then she got some newspaper and drew a pattern on it from the shirt. As I cut it out, I noticed it wasn't last week's, as I'd supposed, but the new one. I never bothered with them much; nor did Emmi, but I didn't know if Andras and Auntie were still reading it. I pointed to the date, and Emmi's reaction said it was hard luck if they were. So I went on cutting.

*What with finding spare bits of material, and cutting out and
sewing, it was afternoon before I knew. I wouldn't have thought to
stop and eat if Emmi hadn't made me. I didn't want to, at first,
in case I felt sick again, but she seemed to think I wouldn't, and
that it was important, so I trusted it to be all right, and it was.*

*I couldn't wait to get back to the little shirt. Auntie was back by
then, but she was too interested in passing on gossip to Emmi to
notice what I was working on. It took me a long time, because I
wanted to get all the stitches really, really small and straight, just
right, like the others had been. And then there was this pretty bit
of braid Emmi'd found me in her work box, to put on the front.
But I got it finished before it was time to start making supper. It
was really hard not to shout: "Done it!" or something. I nearly held
it up for Emmi to see, but her laugh and little shake of the head
reminded me about Auntie, and I still didn't want anyone else to
know before him.*

*When we went out to the kitchen, I took it with me, and she had
a close look, smiled, and signed "beautiful". I got a bit emotional
for some reason and hugged her. It felt like she was taken by surprise, at first, but after a moment she relaxed and held me. It was
just then that we heard Andras at the door.*

*I had a moment of panic. Suppose I tell him and it all goes
wrong; he'd be so upset? I looked up at Emmi, wondering how to
get it across, but I think it was in my eyes already. She just pointed to the stairs, and as I went up I heard her tell Andras to follow
me.*

"Oh God, Anni. That's fantastic. It's the best ever. Are you
certain?"

"Well, Emmi seems to be. I mean, I don't know much about
it really, but I told her how everything was, and she doesn't
think there's any doubt. I trust her. Look, I made this today."

"That's *tiny*. Is the baby really going to be as small as that?"

She laughed. "Well, it's the same size yours was."

I spread the thing on the palms of my hands, trying to imagine holding someone small enough to fit into it, and a shiver
went all through me, not fear exactly but like I felt when the
priest said we were married.

"How long till ...?"

"March or April, I think. I'm not sure exactly when I have to count from. There's all sorts of things I'm not sure of; I need you to ask Mum or Emmi for me."

"It's only six-and-a-half months.... We'll be able to talk to each other anywhere again. You'll be able to sing to him."

"Oh, it's a him, is it?"

"It doesn't seem right to say *it,* that's all.... I don't mind which it is, truly I don't. I'm just so glad it's happened. We've got to tell your folks."

"You have, yes."

"You can still do it, if you want. I'll bring them back here and you can sign it."

She laughed again. "Do you think they won't know as soon as they see your face? Go and tell them how clever you've been."

I took her back downstairs and hugged my mother, and left them telling Auntie while I ran to Marti's. He looked a bit alarmed to see me on the doorstep out of breath, but Anni was right; as soon as he saw the excitement in my face, he knew. He shushed me and called Hanna, so they could hear it together. Then I had to tell Ria and the lads, (she just raised an eyebrow and said something offhand, but the boys kept calling each other Uncle Stevi and Uncle Nico and falling about laughing). And Hanna got it through to Bapa with signs mostly, and everyone had to hug me, and when I got my breath back, I took the whole lot of them down the road to our place.

They all squeezed in to the little front room, and hugged Anni (though I noticed Marti took rather more care of her ribs than he had of mine), and you never heard so many people talking at once. My mother and Hanna were talking stuff I could hardly understand, and what I did grasp sounded dead embarrassing, but Anni looked as if she was following it closely. They seemed to be agreed the baby was due in late March sometime, and she counted the months off on her fingers for Bapa. He looked perkier than I'd seen him in weeks; the cooler weather agreed better with him, but it was more than that. I could see him thinking: only a few more months and she'd be speaking again: not to him, admittedly, but he'd be able to hear her talk and sing to me and the baby – if he still had any hearing by then. I could see him thinking that, too.

People kept congratulating me, but I didn't feel proud so much as lucky. When I thought of the baby, I was mostly just thinking of her being able to speak to me in public again; of me being able to hear her voice whenever I wanted. That was really the main reason I'd wanted a baby at all, just to make that happen. If I thought of an actual person filling that little shirt, it gave me an odd feeling I didn't understand and wasn't sure I liked much. I preferred to think about her. I still wished she could have told them, heard them congratulate her in words, joined in with all this chat. But she looked much more part of things than she had done lately. I'd seen her, when folk came around; so detached, on the edge, almost like Bapa. She wasn't like that now. It wasn't that she looked happy all the time – in fact, when she wasn't remembering to smile, I could see she was preoccupied, worried even. But she didn't look as if she was about to drift away from us any more.

11

HANNA; ANNI

Of course I had to spend a lot more time round at their place, not that it was any hardship. She needed me and Emmi to talk about it; give her some idea what was in store. It took me back, all that reminiscing.

"What did you do for the sickness? I used to eat dry bread, as soon as I woke up. That generally helped."

Emmi grimaced. "Not sure I wouldn't rather be sick. I used to drink tea, I think. How long before yours cleared up?"

"Not long with most of them, but the first time was worst; it went on not far short of three months. But after that, I felt wonderful. I was never healthier."

Just not retching every morning must make you feel fairly healthy.

"Tomas's Lena told me," piped up Auntie, "she was sick the whole way through."

I think I'll go down to the river.

"Oh, I'm sure she was exaggerating. It isn't that bad for anyone." Every time Auntie opened her mouth I was on edge; she knew nothing about it herself, of course, but she had all the tales from others and she never seemed to think how they might frighten Anni. I used to worry about what she might be saying to Emmi in front of her, when I wasn't there.

Anni was knitting a little hat in various colours, from odd ends of wool. She was quicker at it than I remembered. I could see her looking up sometimes, following our faces, and her fingers still going. She still dropped stitches now and then, though.

"Oh no; it is sometimes; it can go on for the whole nine months..." Auntie was still at it.

"Well, I hope it did for Lena", said Emmi, "because I can't stand the woman. But you know what she's like; she won't be outdone by anyone. I'm only surprised she didn't claim she had it for eighteen months."

It was unkind; I hate catty remarks normally, but it did make Anni smile with her eyes – nearly laugh, in fact – so perhaps that's why Emmi said it. I'd have said almost anything myself, to ease her worries.

I knew some of them, because Andras had told me. Why couldn't she feel it yet; how would she know if it was dead? What did she have to do, or not do, to avoid harming it? She was terrified of miscarrying.

Whenever he asked me something, I'd give him the answer for her, or go across myself, if he was on the way to work and couldn't get home for a while. But some things I didn't like talking about in front of Auntie, in case she started on her scary tales. I'd have to snatch a moment alone with Emmi, and hope things would get passed on by signs. It used to drive me mad sometimes, thinking of her longing to know something, and maybe having to wait until Andras got home.

Of course, when he was in, she could get him to ask Emmi things, and I knew he did; but sometimes he seemed to be less embarrassed asking me. He'd pop in before work, to tell me how she was, he said, but generally there'd be some question too. If I said: "Have you asked Emmi?", he'd come back with something about wanting to make sure, because after all I'd had four.... Which was true enough. Thinking about him reminded me of something I wanted to say.

"Marti says Andras is working really hard these days; you can see he takes the whole thing seriously. But I hope he doesn't let it get too much for him; he should take a break from it all sometimes, too."

Emmi raised an eyebrow. "Dear me, yes; it must be hell for men.... He gets down the Eagle once a week or so with Jos and the lads; I don't see he's got much to complain of."

"Oh, that's good."

Emmi winked at Anni. "We shoo him out, so we can get on with things." She gestured at the crib in the corner; she was hemming a little sheet for it. Anni laughed silently and returned her look; for a moment their eyes were very alike.

"I wish I'd kept more of our stuff, after Nico.... But there never seems to be enough space for things. I gave most of it to my sisters. I'm sewing away now though, whenever there's a minute spare; it's nice to work on something little, instead of Marti's shirts."

He'll have enough clothes for an army, at this rate; everyone wants to make something..... Damn. I should have done that row in rib.

She was looking quite chirpy; she was better when we were talking. Just now and then, her brow would furrow, or she'd twist a finger in her veil, and I'd wonder what was going through her mind, and how I could get to it to put things right. Often, all you could do was help her think of something else.

"We've got a visitor coming, next month: our niece from the city."

Gina? I haven't seen her in ages.

"Adam's Gina? Haven't seen her in ages. She doesn't get back much, does she?"

"Well, it isn't really home for her; she was so young when they moved. When she was smaller she used to like coming to stay with us in summer, but the attraction of swimming and picking blackberries wore off long since. Marti saw her in the city last year; he says she's very much the young lady. She asked to stay the month in her letter, though. I was quite surprised."

She'll be here when the singer comes back. Whose house this time? I wish it could be here, but you could never get everyone into this little place. It used to be mine – my old house – sometimes.

I wish I could be there, hear the singing, join in with it, even under my breath, even through this. I wish the baby could hear it through me. I wonder if they can do that; hear things from in there? If he did, and it was the first thing she ever heard, and he moved in time to it and I felt her....

I wonder if the songs will sound any different, without my voice? No: why should they? Voices come and go every year; who's going to notice?

Next year; next year I'll be there, with the baby, and I'll breathe the words to... did I say "him" or "her", last time?

I shouldn't say either. "It" would be better. It's all unlucky, this: telling myself it's real, it's a person already, giving it names, knitting it hats, dreaming its face. I could still lose it. Don't get attached; don't get your hopes up.

She'd stopped looking from face to face; she was staring down at her knitting and her needles were jabbing furiously at it. I went back over what I'd said, but I couldn't think what was upsetting her. I glanced at Emmi to see if she had a clue, but her eyes were fixed on Anni too. Change the subject, I thought; make her think of something else... I looked round at Auntie, still busy with her birds' eggs. She'd just finished one and was turning it around in her hand.

"That's a lovely blue. Did you paint it?"

"No, they're like that to start with. I just varnished it and stuck the glittery bits on; it's supposed to be a raindrop, see..."

No it isn't; it's a songthrush, a bloody songthrush, at least it would have been if it had ever had a chance.

She looked more and more agitated the more we spoke. I thought: I must say something. I can't leave it like this.

"Anni's looking well. Is everything going as it should?"

"Very much so. She can't eat much in the morning still, but I see she makes up for it later, and she's eating all the right things. She walks in the garden when the weather's fit; rests when she's tired; we don't let her stretch up for things or carry anything heavy. She can't even go up or down the stairs without Andras or me there; we're not taking any chances on falls."

I laughed out loud. "Why, even Marti wasn't such a tyrant as that! And his mother expected me to do my share around the house practically until I was giving birth, and nothing went wrong with any of them."

"No harm in keeping busy: Anni does enough. But no risks. Nothing's *going* to go wrong, and there's no reason it should."

She talked as if she wouldn't let it. Anni was looking up again, following what we said, and I thought her eyes smiled.

Auntie cleared her throat, and my heart sank.

"It's all in God's hands; we can never tell. Poor Mina..." I was pretty sure Anni didn't know about her, and I was trying to think how to interrupt without being rude, but Emmi was quicker.

"No, of course not. We don't know we'll be here tomorrow

73

morning, but if we didn't suppose so, we wouldn't be much use to anyone. And I didn't know Jon was going to die at twenty-nine, but when he did, I knew I could get over it, if I had to."

It was very unusual to hear her speak of Jon so directly; she seldom mentioned him by name at all. I was a bit startled, and even Auntie subsided into silence. Anni's eyes were fixed on Emmi. They looked big and troubled, but for the first time since I'd come in, it looked more as if she was concerned for someone else. Not that I'm blaming her for being wrapped up in her own problems; the way she was placed, anyone could excuse that.

The clock on the wall chimed, and Emmi looked up in surprise.

"He'll be home soon. What's happened to the afternoons, these days? No, don't go yet. You can stay a bit longer, can't you?"

"Well, Marti won't be far behind him.. but... oh, Ria can get things ready perfectly well without me; I just don't like to admit it sometimes."

She started getting supper ready, and Anni went at once to help. I joined them in the kitchen, and we all clattered about in the cramped space while Emmi and I took the chance to tell each other what we thought of lurid old wives' tales about childbirth. I'd forgotten how ridiculous some of them were. We were laughing soon; her too, silently of course. I realised suddenly that I hadn't heard her hum under her breath in weeks. Once she reached up to the plate cupboard, not thinking. Emmi caught her hands and drew them back down, with a shake of the head. But she was smiling too, and Anni signed "sorry" looking up from under her eyelashes, full of mischief.

Emmi pointed back into the front room, trying to look stern, and Anni grinned under the veil and went back to her knitting. We'd nearly got everything done anyway; he got back a bit later than we expected.

They were together in an instant, kissing and hugging, while Auntie looked on clicking her tongue: young folk probably didn't do that with anyone watching, in her day. Well, times change, and there's never too much kindness. He looked tired.

"Was there a lot of work on?" I asked.

"Oh, not specially, but something came in late. And I'm a provider now; I need the work." He took her back to the chair and settled cushions round her.

I was on the brink of saying something like: it isn't just about providing, the baby'll need to see you at home too – before I remembered how little he'd known of Jon. I was horrified when I thought how it would have sounded, and when he asked me to stay, I said no, it was time I was going, which was true anyway.

I was just picking up my knitting, when Anni finished the little hat and waved it in the air. She showed it to him first, and perched it on his head, then gave it to Emmi, who looked it all over and then held it out to me. "Look, isn't it sweet?"

It was, too: a couple of little flaws, but she obviously didn't propose to notice them. She stroked Anni's cheek, smiling. I said goodbye and went home. I caught myself hoping, meanly, that when I got there, I'd find there was something they hadn't been able to manage without me.

12

Anni: Andras

"Andras"

"Mm?"

"My breasts have gone peculiar."

"They look fine to me. This bit's fine, and that bit's fine, and...."

"No, stop it, listen; they feel really heavy and they ache, and they've gone all brown here, see, and these little blue lines weren't there before."

"Yeah, I like them; they're pretty."

"*Stop it...* I need to know if it's meant to happen; suppose it isn't, and I can't feed the baby? Ask Emmi for me?"

"Oh, bloody hell! I can't ask her something like that... all right, all right, I'm sorry. I know you need me to. I'll ask, I promise. I'll find a way. Maybe if I stare in the opposite direction and say it very quickly...."

"Look, a few months ago I wouldn't have believed *I* could say things like that to *you*, but it doesn't bother me now. It doesn't bother you, does it?"

"No.... no, it feels right. Natural. It's just with my mother... her and all that stuff just doesn't seem to go together."

"Well, she must have gone through it with you. And talked to your dad about it."

"I can't imagine that."

"Does it hurt you to hear people talk about him?"

"No. I wish people would. I wish *she* would. I can hardly remember him, you know. His face, just a little bit, and of course there's that photograph, but never his voice, nor anything he did."

"Didn't she tell you about him when you were little?"

"Never unless I asked, and not much then."

"Well, what about *his* family? They must have talked about him."

"Oh, my uncles would tell me things about when he was a boy, yes. It was better than nothing; it made him less of a shadow. But it didn't make him *mine*; it didn't tell me what he was like with her and me."

"You should ask her again, if it means that much to you. She's all right, Emmi; I'm sure she'd talk if she thought it was making you unhappy."

"Yeah, well, maybe I'll keep to one embarrassing subject at a time."

"I like that photograph. It's so like you."

"Well, I can't see it. The hair's darker, and he looks a good bit taller than me."

"Yes, but that sort of thing isn't what makes people look alike.... He's got the same smile as you, sort of lopsided, and you can see his hair flops around in front just like yours."

"Thanks."

"Gina used to like your hair, remember? Is it tomorrow she gets here?"

"No; I meant to tell you. Hanna said she'd written; she'd been delayed somehow but she'll be here next week. The same night the singer comes, so I don't suppose you'll see her straight away."

"You going?"

"Not if you don't want me to."

"I don't mind. You can sing for me. Just don't start fancying any girls."

"Now why should I do that?"

"Well, you might fancy spending time with someone who didn't keep getting sick or have a lump where her waist should be.... Or who went out and met people and did interesting things and had lots to talk about."

"I love you. I won't ever want anyone else. And I'd just as soon stay here, honest. I'll be tired after work and I can do without all that caterwauling; it won't sound half as good without you anyway."

"Oh, you... you're gorgeous sometimes, you know that? But you should go; everyone'll be there, and it'd look odd if you weren't. And you can tell me all about it. You spend too much time at work anyway. Tell Dad he mustn't keep you so late."

"That'd go down well. I can hear him now..."

"Speaking to you today, was he?"

"Oh, don't tease... I should never have told you about that. We haven't had so much as a disagreement in ages. Of course, that might be because I keep quiet when I disagree with him, like I did today."

"What about?"

"Only Edo. His brother's in the shop now, learning the ropes, and when he can manage on his own the old man'll let Edo leave. It looks as if he really will come this time. Marti thinks it'll all work out fine."

"Why are you so sure it won't?"

"I'm not, but I've got a hell of a bad feeling about it."

"It's this ritual thing with the lads, isn't it?"

"Partly. I'm not sure he can be part of a group anyway, but yes, that really worries me."

"You must have gone through it, and you managed. Was it really that scary?"

"Well, I wasn't alone, for a start; me and Jos joined the same day, so we went through it together. That helped a bit. But yes, I was scared. I didn't know what they were going to do, but I knew it wasn't meant to be enjoyable. I didn't know when, either; it doesn't happen until work's nearly over, but no-one tells you that, so I was on edge all day. When they finally grabbed me, I think it was almost a relief – to start with, anyway."

"What *do* they do?"

"I don't want to talk about most of it; I really don't. No, don't look so horrified; it isn't that awful. Anyway it's only the last bit that stays with you. Most of the rest is just humiliating, and maybe painful now and then, but it wouldn't sound fearsome if I told you, just a bit daft. The fear comes from not knowing for certain how far they'll go."

"Oh come on, Dad wouldn't let anything really bad happen."

"He isn't there; he makes damn sure of it. It's just you and them, that's the whole point. You're keyed up anyway; there's

78

one of you and four of them, plus the rest standing around egging them on, and it doesn't feel like a joke between friends for long. Plus there's generally some bastard like Simo now, who enjoys it too much. When I joined, it was Eric; remember him?

"Susi's big brother Eric, that went to the army? He always seemed nice enough."

"He would have been, around the boss's family. But anything he had any power over, from the yard dogs upwards, needed to watch out. I hope they never promote him. When there's four guys swinging you over a mastering pit full of hot water and assorted shit, it doesn't help if the face you happen to look up into has a grin on it that says he'd as soon drop you as not."

"*Yeuch!* They don't, do they?"

"No, not unless you struggle so much they can't help it. Nor in the leaching pits with the tanning liquors. But then they move on again; they're carrying you face up, so all you can see is the sky and their faces, and the next thing you smell is lime."

"Oh no... not the lime pits? They wouldn't risk swinging anyone over those, surely? Wouldn't even the one with the weakest solution burn you?"

"I should think so. The thought certainly crosses your mind at the time. Your first instinct is to struggle free, and then you realise you can't, because that'll *make* them drop you, whether they want to or not. You have to keep still and trust them. I had a moment of blind panic, when I first smelt the lime, and I looked from face to face. And something cleared in my head suddenly; the two who had me by the ankles were brothers and uncles of friends of mine; I'd known them all my life, and I just all at once *knew* they would never do anything to really hurt me. Then I thought: Eric might, and as soon as I thought it, I knew *he* couldn't, either, because they'd never let him. There are folk like him wherever you work, but in a decent yard the others hold them back; no-one's bigger than the group. It was the most unspeakable relief. I just lay back and grinned at them."

"But what if they dropped someone by accident?"

"He'd get wet, wouldn't he! It isn't one of the lime pits at all; it's the big water pit right next to them. Remember, you're the wrong way up to see it; whatever you recall about the layout of the yard has gone to hell by then; you smell the lime when you pass the pits, and your imagination does the rest. You're never in danger for a moment."

"What a daft carry-on! I don't know; lads just don't grow up somehow.... So you could tell Edo all that, beforehand?"

"If I did, and the lads found out, I wouldn't be exactly popular. Anyway, do you think I'd be doing him any favours?"

"Well, he wouldn't be so scared."

"Maybe not, but he'd never learn that he doesn't *have* to be. I tell you, Anni, something happened in my head when I realised that, and it wouldn't have, if I'd known from the start that the lime wasn't below. To have trusted someone completely like that, even just for a few moments, makes a hell of a difference, and maybe it would for him."

"Yes, I can see that.... if he can."

"That's what I'm not sure about."

"I hate Ossi. Most of this is his fault, you know."

"Yeah, I suppose. I wonder how hard it is. To bring up a child right, I mean."

"Well, if we just love him and don't hit her and shout at him all the time, we've got to be doing better than Ossi."

"You still doing that? Does it really stop you thinking of a him or a her?"

"Mostly.... I can't help thinking of a little copy of you, sometimes."

"God help him.... What did Marti do when any of you did something bad?"

"Left Mum to sort it out... No, that's not fair; he told us off or punished us if he had to, but he never hit any of us, and he never got angry; he'd walk away rather than do that. I never even *saw* him angry until that time poor Barbara's husband hit her in the street and Dad held him against the wall with one hand and told him what he thought about it. I was shattered; he was so calm, icy calm...."

"I know; I've seen him. But he never got like that with you?"

"No. The worst he ever did with us was tell us he was disappointed. Don't laugh; it really hurts to disappoint someone you love. I feel sorry for Stevi sometimes, because he gets more of that. Dad can't understand why he isn't keener on school."

"Oh, my mother was just the same. Parents are funny like that. Do they totally *forget* what it was like, or what? Hell, how long before our kid is saying that about us?"

"It's got to be born first. I don't want to think beyond that. It might be unlucky."

"Hey, don't worry. It'll be fine. All right, I don't know that, but you don't know any reason it shouldn't be, either. Think happy. Hanna says it can feel your mood. She reckons that's why you sing so much, because she was so happy all the time she was carrying you."

"She's as soft as you are."

"She's nice. I really get on with her."

"I've noticed. So has Emmi."

"What do you mean?"

"I've seen how she looks sometimes, when you two are chatting or when you say: Hanna said such-and-such, or Mum talks about you. I think she feels a bit edged out sometimes."

"Oh, come on, I thought she might be jealous of *you*, when we got together, but that's never happened... has it?"

"No, never. But I've never tried to be your mother. I think Mum does, sometimes. It probably comes natural to her; she's had four after all.... But you're all Emmi's got. I'd understand it, if she was a bit jealous."

"Wow. I've got women fighting over me. I could get to like this... stop it! Don't hit me... it's not fair; you know I can't do a thing to you. How did you get to be so violent, with such a gentle upbringing? I hope you're not going to be like that with our child."

"It'll be so small. I'm going to be scared to hold him; scared every time she cries. Why do they make them so fragile?"

"I know. I'm scared too. One time I hurt your hand by accident and I was really afraid to touch you afterwards. I felt so big and clumsy, and this is worse. I feel as if every time I say or do the wrong thing, I'll wreck its chances."

"No, you won't... Mum and Dad weren't perfect; I don't suppose Emmi was either. And look what brilliant results they got."

13

THE SINGER

Ever since the company started arriving, the air in this place hasn't been right. It's the men, or at least the ones who work in that bloody tanyard; I can smell the chemicals off them. Lime; it never quite washes off, and that dust they seem to take everywhere. I swear I can feel it at the back of my throat. It makes me edgy; anything wrong in my throat and I can feel chills all down my spine. The thought of losing my voice, of maybe having to settle down and do a proper job of work, like them... no, forget it, I'd go down to the river first.

Who did I sing to here, last time? Oh God, Redlips, her with the black curls all down her back and the lovely voice. Can't see her. Another one gone quiet. I still recall how she looked at that lad. Wonder if *he's* here – all the men look alike to me, or at least they don't stay in my memory.

But my little choirs of girls, in villages and towns up and down the country, I don't forget them. They change all the time: a voice that started reedy and childlike will warm up and deepen, I hear it a little different each time, and then just when it's perfect it disappears, and new ones come in, and the whole sound of the group is just that bit altered. I read once that sometimes the stars grow old and flicker out, so that the clusters we see aren't the same as in olden days. But that would take hundreds of years, whereas in my little clusters, stars go out all the time. And nobody misses them, much, because there are always new voices and faces to follow them. In a few years, nobody remembers a hair colour, or the shape of a mouth or chin, or a voice like icy water. Except me. I don't forget one face or voice; if I close my eyes I can see them all pass by, and hear each one sing, all my silent stars.

I've found one to sing to here, with a pale face and very straight, blue-black hair like a magpie's tail, but I can't really concentrate on her yet; I'm still thinking of Redlips. It always takes me a while to get my mind off the last one, and stop resenting the others for still being there when she isn't. I started off with the crane song, and I could still hear her voice soaring in it. Poor Magpie was no bloody substitute.

I wish I knew where she was. At home, most like, but if this *is* her home now, she could be upstairs or in the next room, listening. And I know she probably isn't, but just in case, I can't help singing one for her:

> The ground is frozen,
> the sky is grey.
> I remember
> when it was May.
>
> Bluebells sleeping
> under the snow.
> In my mind
> they sway and glow,
>
> just as they did
> when last I met you.
> How could you think
> I would forget you?

Or you, or you, or you... I smile at Magpie, raise my hand a little as if to draw more voice out of her. It's got promise; she just needs a bit more confidence in it.

One of the men calls out, a bit slurred: "Do us *Blackweir River*, man". And I cringe, and pretend I haven't heard, but some others take it up. The customer is always right. Ignorant, tasteless and maudlin, but right.

I hate that song. It's a real bloke's song, for a start, and a drunken one at that, the kind you sing down the pub when you're smashed and sorry for yourself. It's got no subtlety, in the words or the music, and if it had, the men who sing it wouldn't notice; they just bawl it out as loud as possible and howl into their beer. The girls hardly bother to sing it and I don't blame them. Let's just do the damn thing and get it over with.

When the snow turned into rain,
that's when I came home again

– why he couldn't just say "in Spring", God knows. They're well away already, swaying and slurring the words. Magpie's lips are twitching as if she wants to laugh. She's got a humorous mouth; I hadn't noticed before. I wink at her and she grins back. At least I don't have to work at leading this, they all know it backwards.

Looked all round; she wasn't there.
Couldn't see her anywhere.

I just hope none of them breaks down. Quite often, there's some lad it's personal for. I've got my eye on one slightly off on his own, who looks as if he might want to make a drama out of it. He sings flat, too.

Where are we? Oh, the bit where the gutless wonder sends his pal to the girl's house.

Ask her kin, dear friend, please do:
ask them what I'm scared to know.

Say the words that must be said:
is she wed or is she dead?

– and they roar it out, just where the girls would have had the sense to drop their voices to a whisper.

If she's wed another man,
I'll go down to Blackwall town.

How to drown her memory?
Find a pub and drink it dry.

Well, that's one answer, I suppose. It was my dad's answer to most things, as I recall. The girls are chatting amongst themselves; Magpie's playing with a half-grown cat, and it makes me think of Redlips and the black kitten. I tend to remember cats better than men, too.

They're building up to the big finale. I must try not to put my hands over my ears when they bellow the last line.

If she's dead and gone for ever,
I'll go down to Blackweir River.

How to drown her memory?
RIVER, RIVER, OVER ME...

God, how maudlin can you get? They're all loving it, really enjoying the misery. Well, maybe not the young one with the lousy voice. He's gone very white and his mouth's trembling. Sod it, I've had enough of this. I grab the guitar and send out one long, high, ringing note that stops them all in their tracks, and then go straight into a fast one with a lot of complicated harmonies in it. One for me and the girls. They come alive in an instant and fix all their attention on me; taking it in, giving it back.

Oh Magpie, Redlips, Rowanhair: all my laughing mouths, my lit faces, my voices here today and gone tomorrow... I see you as plain as the man in the song sees the bluebells in winter. And I feel such a pang for all those faces and voices that moved me so much at the time.

I wonder if they would have hurt me so beautifully, if I'd thought they'd last for always? I wonder if that's what gives it an edge, knowing it'll soon be gone? Like I sense the places I'm in more, because I know I might not see them again for months, or years, or ever. The girls in the big city, where the custom's died out; do I feel the same about them? I don't know... I don't think so, and yet they're gone just as fast, moving on to new work in a new place, or following some man who is. People are getting more like me every year.

There's a city girl here tonight, visiting kin, I suppose, but I'm sure she wasn't brought up here. It isn't just the clothes. She's looking at everything from outside, and faintly amused by it. That includes me, irritatingly enough; she's singing, but not with the passion of the others, not intent on my face to get it dead right. More indulging the country cousins by singing along with these tired old favourites. It makes me mad, because

86

of course I wouldn't be doing this stuff in town; I sing her sort of thing just as well and I can do the same to city girls as I do here; I could have you on a string, darling, no trouble... She still knows all the words, though, and fusses over the cats and flirts with the lads, just like the rest of them.

There's a lad Magpie looks across at, now and again. I watch for that: *make my stars go out, would you, you little....* There's nothing special about him; he's just like all the rest, just like that one Redlips looked at as if there were no-one remotely like him in the world. Magpie doesn't though, not quite. He's crazy for her; you can see that, but she looks at him different somehow. Like she likes him, but she's thinking about it; not as if she couldn't live without him. *Don't let him talk you round, love; you're the only one you can't live without, believe me.*

I want to hear her voice on its own again. It's growing on me. Sing this one with me. Not *for* me; just with me. But not for him, either. Sing it just for you. I chose it for you; it's got some humour. You'll like it.

I sign the others quiet and play the intro. She knows it; gives me a little nod. It's a courtship-and-answer song: I sing her the first verse:

Hawk in the tree; hawk in the tree,
come to my wrist and stay with me.

And she gives me back the answer, clear and sharp, with a lovely half-laugh in the voice:

Why should I come; why should I come,
How would it serve me, to leave my home?

You go on thinking that way, darling.

I'll feed you well; I'll feed you well,
from my own hand you'll eat your fill.

But I can hunt; but I can hunt.
I can kill all the food I want.

I've built a house, spacious and fair.
Come and live there; come and live there.

Every morning when I wake up, there's that moment, halfway between asleep and awake, when I think: where the hell am I today? Best moment of the day, that is.

See the wide sky I wander in?
All of it mine; all of it mine.

I'll give you bells, silver and sweet,
silk round your feet; silk round your feet.

And she throws all that long fall of hair back and sings it out:

Who would choose bonds, when they had none?
Watch me, I'm gone; watch me, I'm gone.

Watch me, I'm gone.... I watch you every year, and you're gone. I hear that last lovely flight in your voices before they come back to earth and get mewed up. Every spring and autumn I think: this one's different; she won't come down. But you do; you all do. If I didn't keep moving on, I couldn't stand it.

I'd go on singing all night, if you'd sing with me, but tomorrow's Sunday; these folk have church to go to. They know better than to wake me up for that, now. I'll get up when I feel like it. If they're back, they'll offer me food, and I'll eat, and they'll ask me to stay another night, and I'll say thanks, but I have to get to such-and-such a place. And they won't argue; they know me.

Or if I wake a bit earlier and they're still in church, I might just slip off. They don't take offence at that either. Sometimes they leave food for me to eat or take with me; I quite like it that way. I'll maybe sit in the garden a while, in the air they call chill but which seems warm enough to me, drinking the coffee they've left and watching the leaves fall, each one detaching from the tree so easily, no big scenes or goodbyes. And then off into the little country roads where hardly anyone's about yet, and when they come back, they'll find the cup washed up – I'm tidy like that; comes of having no woman around – and a note on the table. Watch me, I'm gone.

14

GINA; ANNI

I really wonder if I should have come at all. I did think twice about it; the theatres had just started up again and town's so lively this time of year; just being away for a week, you seem to miss so much. But I didn't want to disappoint Aunt Hanna, and to be honest, I wasn't sorry to get out of the house either.

I hadn't counted on arriving the same night as the ballad-singer. That's a big event, out in these little places, the only entertainment they get in months, so of course the whole village goes along. They were amazed that I went, though. Everyone I met was exclaiming; *all that way by train; you must be exhausted*, and Aunt Hanna offered to stay at home with me if I was too tired to go! I couldn't help laughing. They'll do a full day's work and think nothing of it, but sit on a train for a few hours and they treat you as if you'd climbed a mountain.

Not that I was particularly wild to hear all those old songs again: I heard enough of them in my childhood, but I wasn't having them think a little journey had tired me out, and it was a chance to see everyone again. Or so I thought.

I knew Anni had married, of course; Uncle Marti had told me so when he came to town, months back. And when I asked the news, the first thing Aunt Hanna told me was that the baby was on the way. They all seemed really delighted about it, and of course I was too; not that I'd fancy being tied down quite so young, but it's different out here; it's not as if there's much else a girl can do.... And I remembered Andras a little bit from way back, when I was a child and used to come for the summer. Not much, because he was a few years older than us, but he was always kind.

So when we crowded into the room where the singer would perform, and Andras came up and said hello, the first thing I said was: "Where's Anni?" And he looked taken aback a moment, and said: "At home". And I still didn't get it. I asked if she was ill, and he fidgeted with his hair, the bit that always fell forward over his face, and said: "No.. no, she's quite well, considering..." and suddenly discovered something urgent he needed to talk to Uncle Marti about.

I turned to Aunt Hanna; I suppose I must have looked baffled.

"I'm sorry, Gina. I should have reminded you, but I thought you'd remember."

My mother had said, just before I left: "Don't tread on any toes there, now. Remember, they still keep to the old ways." I thought she meant the veil. My mother still veils her hair out of doors, but not her face; hardly anyone in town does, these days.

It hadn't even crossed my mind that she could have meant the other thing. A bride not going out for – what was it? A year? And not *speaking* to anyone – oh no, they surely weren't still keeping *that* up?

"Well, yes." Aunt Hanna sounded embarrassed, which I couldn't wonder at. They should all be embarrassed – honestly, we might never have left the Dark Ages.

"What's Andras thinking of, putting her through this? I used to really like him."

"Well, now, he didn't invent it. He gets very impatient with it actually; he can't wait to be able to speak freely to her again."

"Then why doesn't he just do it? Who could stop him? How are ridiculous old habits like this ever going to die out if someone doesn't put a stop to them?"

Aunt Hanna looked awfully uncomfortable and I recalled how much she hated arguments. Normally, nothing would have stopped me speaking my mind, but she'd always been kind to me. I liked her a lot, and she couldn't help being of her time. So I let it drop. But I did manage to whisper to Ria: "I hope *you're* not planning to go along with that nonsense." She didn't say anything; just gave me that cool little smile of hers, but I'm sure *she* sees the stupidity of it.

The evening was actually less of a bore than I'd feared it might be. It's nice, now and again, to do something really unsophisticated. Of course it didn't compare with hearing a trained choir sing at a proper concert, but on the other hand, it was a real novelty to sing myself, for a change! I'd forgotten how enjoyable it is to actually make a sound yourself, even a mediocre one. I haven't got much of a voice at all, but in a crowd it doesn't seem to matter. It was amusing to watch the singer, as well; he'd obviously spent his life thinking girls couldn't resist him. Out in these remote places, of course, he's a star. He didn't have a bad voice, actually, but totally untrained of course. It suited those naive old songs. I was surprised how many of the words I recalled.

We used to spend whole summers here, when I was little. Dad liked to show us where he'd sledged down hills and picked blackberries. He'd go off fishing for hours with Uncle Marti and come back brown and laughing, vowing the business could go hang and he'd never go back to the city again. And of course my brothers and I would be all for it, because at that age the country seems like paradise, but my mother would look really anxious in case he meant it. I can sympathise now.

Dad took my brothers fishing too, sometimes, but I hated it – I can't stand that slimy look fish have, and the way they flop around in the air. Anni and Ria had no time for it either, because it meant staying quiet, so we were often together. Anni was just about my age, and we did all the usual things: played at cooking and created chaos in Aunt Hanna's kitchen, took the dogs out, got stuck up trees.... And then when we were a bit older it was crushing berries to paint our lips, comparing diaries, and making up boyfriends to put in them – at least it was for me and Anni; Ria was inclined to mock at that, but then she was a little younger.

I really knew Anni then, or I'd thought I did. And I hadn't been back for about five years, what with one thing and another, so in my mind she was still that girl, with the curly hair and the mischievous streak, who was always singing something. Just a little older, like me: the same but a few years older.

When we went round there on the Sunday, Aunt Hanna looked apprehensive and I reassured her: "It's all right; I understand now. I was just off guard last night, but I'm prepared now." And I really meant it: I thought I was.

But then when Andras let us in, and we said hello to him and his mother and the old lady, and then this other woman came over and hugged Aunt Hanna and Ria, and then turned to me, and Andras said: "Anni says hello too"....

I think my jaw dropped. She was dressed like all the others, except for the long silver sleeveless coat. (You still see those in town sometimes, at the more traditional weddings.) Her waist had thickened, of course, but that wouldn't have mattered; it wouldn't have made her not Anni. It was all the things that weren't there – the hair, the mouth, the chin, all hidden; just a pair of eyes looking out of blackness like all the others; just like all the others. I just gaped at her and said: "Oh, Anni!"

I couldn't help it; I didn't mean to embarrass anyone. She looked down, and then away, at Andras and then at his mother, as if for help. Andras seemed totally at a loss – I'd forgotten how brown his eyes were, and how worried they could look – but his mother just spoke calmly to me, as if it hadn't happened.

"How are your parents these days? We never see them now."

"My father hasn't been able to get away from work for ages. He asked to be remembered to you, though." The woman I couldn't see Anni in had sat down again and picked up some sewing. That was *one* thing we never did as children; we both hated it.

"Can't be much fun for your mother. What does she do with her time, now you're all grown?"

"Oh, she's always out and about; visiting friends and such, and she knows a lot of the theatre people, so she goes to all the plays. She keeps busy."

I couldn't stop my eyes wandering to Anni. She was glancing from her mother to Ria, and she looked agitated about something – I hoped it wasn't me. Then she looked across to Andras, and he seemed to get some sort of message – God knows how, when he could see so little of her face. He asked Aunt Hanna: "Why didn't you bring Marti and Bapa today; are they still sleeping off last night?"

She laughed. "Marti was a bit the worse for wear, yes: we couldn't even get him up for church. Well we tried, but he growled at us from under the blankets and told us to try again in spring."

Ria nodded and grinned. "Grandfather's just tired. He stayed up as late as anyone; said he'd play at being old in the morning. He's in good health though."

He was another one I could hardly recognise; the deafness had made a great difference to him. I'd wondered, the night before, why he came, because he clearly couldn't make out much of the music and he didn't seem to talk or be talked to much, either. Sometimes Ria or Aunt Hanna would go over and try to get things across to him, but mostly he just sat there watching faces. You'd think it would have made him feel lonely, all that singing and chatting he couldn't be part of, yet he sat on to the end, just as Ria had said. I wasn't so sure about his health as she seemed to be, though; I'd heard him coughing a lot in the night. I nearly said so, but Aunt Hanna asked me something else about my parents at the same moment.

Of course their curiosity was no surprise, but it was awfully inconvenient. Dad hardly came home these days, and when he did, he and Mother were generally arguing. I had no idea whether he'd told Uncle Marti any of that – if he had, there was no sign of it. I had to talk as if everything were normal. I felt as if Andras's mother and Aunt Hanna were trying to tease information out of me; every answer seemed to spark off another question, so I turned to Andras.

"I bet you don't remember when you got my kite out of the tree? All us thirteen-year-olds used to swoon over you."

I got him, though.

He laughed. "They gave it up later, then."

"Oh, I don't know. I think you'd turn a few heads in town, with that lovely smile!"

What's that to you? You come here with your clothes and your hair and your twenty-inch waist and your voice....

"Whenever I've been in the city, I wasn't smiling. I was gawping at the crowds, or scratching my head because I was lost. I must have turned heads all right, but only as a spectacle. I was hopeless."

"Oh, you just hadn't got the hang of it. Everyone talks about crowds and noise, but if you lived there, you wouldn't even notice them. People never seem to mention the good things. Why, we're hardly indoors of an evening, during the season; you can practically go to a play or a concert every week, and some of them are brilliant. This opera we saw last week..."

Stop it. Stop it. You might as well use a knife.

"... and it isn't all grimy streets. We live quite close to a really beautiful park, with trees and flowers and a lake, and everything."

His mother raised one eyebrow. "They have to have special places for those, then?"

Oh, nice one! Thanks, Emmi.

She looked so unhappy, sitting there being left out of things; it was beginning to drive me mad. I suppose I shouldn't have, but then on the other hand how can you sit back and let something wrong go on? I couldn't.

"Look, everyone, this is ridiculous. What possible harm would it do if Anni talked to the rest of us, and we talked to her?"

Go away. Please. Just disappear.

The old lady gave a little shocked squeak, and Aunt Hanna looked concerned. Anni stared furiously at the carpet, as if the pattern were something fascinating. I turned to the others.

"You're not daft enough, or ignorant enough, to agree with this, Andras; you must know it's all but died out. You *all* know that; you too, Anni."

She stood up, not looking at me, and left the room. Andras followed her.

"Why are you all sticking your heads in the sand? I'm right; you know I'm right."

"Well," his mother said, "couldn't you be right *quietly*, without making such an almighty fuss about it?"

"No! You won't get anything *put* right that way."

I looked at Ria for support, but she said nothing, just looked coolly amused. Aunt Hanna was really upset, and I could see I was getting nowhere, so I said no more. We left soon after, and Andras and Anni still hadn't come back.

Aunt Hanna lingered on the doorstep, apologising for me,

no doubt. The thought annoyed me, and I couldn't help saying, when she caught up: "But you have to say what you think's right."

She wiped the back of her hand across her forehead, and I saw it was moist. I never knew anyone who hated a scene so much. In some ways it made a pleasant change – my mother tended to throw ornaments – but sometimes it got on my nerves.

"It's better to be kind than right," she said finally, as if she were sure of that and nothing else.

But it isn't. I know.

15

ANDRAS

Marti brought Edo into the yard, first thing, and handed him over to me.

I was a bit at a loss. When the kids come in straight from school, you generally give them a yard brush and get them sweeping up dogshit for the mastering pit, but Edo was really too old for that. I remembered none of his folks had ever worked in the yard, so I gave him a tour. He was baffled by all the pits.

"See, what we do here is mostly soften things up. The hide comes in raw and hard; if you tried to bend it, it'd crack. And we turn it into stuff you can handle and work; make into something useful. The oak bark does that. Cold water plus oak bark makes tannin, right, and hide soaked in it makes leather? But it has to get used to it little by little, start in a weak solution and move up to stronger ones. That's why so many pits."

He nodded. He was quiet, but at least he seemed to take things in. I took him past the mastering pit, trying not to breathe in, and showed him the gentlefolks' gloves and shoe uppers softening in mixed shit. I showed him the big water pit, where the blood gets washed off the new hides, and the lime pits right next to it – I hoped he'd remember that. He watched, mesmerised, as a new hide went in and the wicked stuff seared the hair straight off. I took him to the beam house, to watch Leo cutting, and he flinched and shaded his eyes as we came back out into the brightness.

"I know; it takes a while for your eyes to adjust. The buildings have to be kept dark or the hide discolours. You get used to it."

I took him through some of the jobs we all did – grinding bark, cutting the offal from the new hides. He listened carefully; he was very anxious to please, but when he tried to do it for me, he'd get nervous and fumbling if I watched, even when

I tried to encourage him. He did all right stacking with me, Jos and Ivo, though, and later with Luc shifting hides in the pits.

I wanted him to get to know us; know he didn't need to be scared of us. When we knocked off around midday, we all sat together and shared what we had. He hadn't brought anything; said he wasn't hungry. We all offered him stuff, but he just insisted politely that he was all right. It didn't surprise me; I remembered being new enough for that smell to make me sick. One more thing you get used to. He listened to the chat, answered if anyone spoke to him, but it never exactly turned into a conversation somehow. Still, there's no harm in listening more than you talk.

In the afternoon, I found him things to do near me, but tried not to watch him, since he seemed best on his own. Anyway I wasn't such good company myself now, because I was thinking of what was coming.

I would have been on edge anyway, whoever it had been. I'm not against it, and I don't regret that it was done to me, but I still hate doing it to others. Admitted, there are some lovely moments, when it clicks in their heads that it's all right, and they relax and grin up at you. I know that feeling so exactly, and it's great to share it again.

But to make that happen, you have to put fear in them first, and that's the part I don't like. I'm not very convincing at it, either. Jos is better, not because he's any meaner than me, but because he's a good actor. I stay in the background and try to keep my face expressionless – they must think I'm a right hard bastard.

Edo was cutting up a hide, separating the butt from the offal, or trying to. I watched him dropping things, nearly cutting himself and jumping when anyone spoke, for as long as I could stand it and then I thought: no, she's right, someone has to....

I went over and grabbed the knife off him. "Not like that! The way I told you. Now listen again, properly this time." I dropped my voice right down. "Listen, Edo, don't be scared of what's going to happen. However it looks, you won't be in any danger. It isn't the way it seems. I'm not meant to tell you that, but it's true. Trust me?" He didn't look much as if he did.

"I swear it; I give you my word. Do you think I'd do anything to really hurt you, or let anyone else do it?" He sized me up, trying to decide whether he did or not. I added: "What would I tell Anni?" That finally brought a faint, watery smile and a shake of the head.

"Good. Do me a favour; don't let on that you know. Try to act scared." He nodded, and I threw him the knife back and walked off.

Nobody seemed to suspect what I'd been doing, thank God. I felt very odd about it. Part of me still said I shouldn't have; that I should have given him the chance to do it right, and the other part said he couldn't, and that I had no choice. I just hoped, for my sake, that he could fake being scared.

Around four, when the light started to go, Marti duly discovered he needed to see a man about something, and left the yard. We made sure Edo was absorbed in whatever he was doing; then Jos gave us the nod and we jumped him.

He was dead nervous; I could feel the tension all up his arm, but then that was natural enough. All the lads had gathered round: Luc and I were holding him while Jos and Ivo painted and kept up a humorous commentary for the audience. (I'd told Anni, finally, that part of it involved getting painted with various vegetable dyes, and she looked relieved and said that didn't sound too bad. Depends what's getting painted, though.) Basically all that was happening to him was humiliation, but that's not nothing, I know. It makes them cry, as often as not – I did, a bit – and nobody thinks the worse of you, as long as you don't completely go to pieces.

Edo didn't cry. He stared straight ahead, trying to blank out what was happening. The two in front of him slapped his face, not hard but teasing him to look at them, and he gave them a glance of pure hatred. The lads were dead impressed; they laughed and cheered and I could see them thinking he was a bit of a hard man after all. I was getting worried; I hoped he hadn't forgotten he was meant to be scared.

When we hauled him over to the pits, I had him by one of

the arms. His face was still set like iron, staring at the sky. We swung him over a leaching pit, laughing and pretending to miss our grip, and got the same stubborn lack of reaction. Now and again he'd look at one face or another; if there was any emotion in his face, it was hate, but mostly it struck me as a determination not to show *anything*. When he looked at me, I dared not show any expression either, but I squeezed his arm. I couldn't tell if it reassured him or not. It was the same story at the mastering pit, give or take the appalling stench. And then we went on again.

When he smelt the lime, his whole body went rigid. We got him to the side of the water pit and tried to swing him over it, and it wasn't easy. There was a terrific resistance. I was relieved; I'd been worried he wouldn't make any pretence of being scared. Then he looked up into my face, and I knew he wasn't pretending.

He believed the lime absolutely, and he believed I'd lied to him. I squeezed his arm again, willing him to remember what I'd told him: *it isn't how it seems.* I even said it with my face, as far as I dared. *Christ, I gave you my word; what more do you want? This is me, Andras, the man Anni married; do you really think I'd do that?* But what his eyes said back was: *I always knew you didn't mean it.* Amongst the bitterness of betrayal there was even a flicker of satisfaction at being proved right. Or maybe I just imagined that.

The lads were urging us to swing him again. I tried to put his face out of my mind and get it over with. Whatever he thought, he'd realise soon enough that panic would do no good.

Only he didn't. Once he started fighting, he certainly went all the way. Even as we were swinging him, he was thrashing like a fish on the line, trying to break our grip. Jos shouted: "Get him back", and we were trying to, when he twisted his head and bit my hand. I lost my hold; so did Luc on his other arm – I suppose that was my fault for unbalancing him – and before we knew it, he was in the pit.

As soon as he hit the water, he screamed and contorted, struggling even more than he had in our hands. I was baffled:

I even touched my hand to the water and tasted it, to see if any lime had somehow got into it. But it was pure water. Then I realised it was all in his mind; he'd been so sure he was going to burn that it never occurred to him to stop panicking and see what had really happened. He could feel the lime on his skin; you could see it. The lads standing around had gone quiet; they stared at him, horrified and fascinated.

Jos looked down at the figure sobbing and convulsing in the water, bumping into the hides or the edge at every turn, and shook his head.

"Jesus Christ," he said. He spat into the water, turned and walked off. Most of the others followed, in little groups, talking in hushed voices like folk at a funeral. I heard the word "gutless" from someone.

Luc and I got him out – he seemed in too much of a panic even to think about it – and tried to convince him he wasn't on fire. I held him, unwillingly, because it seemed the only way to calm him down. Luc said you were meant to slap folk in hysterics, and I was tempted, but it would only have made matters worse. All the time, I was trying to think what it was I'd just seen. It wasn't gutlessness. I was sure of that. I reckoned Edo could take an awful lot of pain and humiliation without response, just to avoid giving folk the satisfaction. He hadn't been like that as a child, which was probably why he got picked on at school, but he was now; he'd become as hard in that respect as anyone could be.

It was something else; the certainty that people would let him down, betray him, hurt him if they got the chance. Whatever trust I thought he had in me had evaporated with a whiff of lime, but he trusted *that* as soon as he smelt it. I've heard of being prepared for the worst, but he expected nothing else, and in his mind it had happened. Whatever burning lime feels like, he knew.

Once he'd calmed down, I told him to go home. I couldn't face talking to him about it; it was too embarrassing. And yet I did feel sorry for him, being the way he was. Anni would have tried to comfort him, and I know I should have. But though I didn't despise him as Jos did, there was something about him I didn't want to be near, either. As if what was wrong with him was something catching; no sense in that, I know. But I couldn't help it.

Most folk had left the yard already, and old Leo the beamsman, who had Marti's key, was itching to lock up. That suited me. So I went down to the river to cool off, and who should be on the bank, doing a quiet bit of fishing, but Marti. I didn't think he'd have gone far. In a better mood, it would have amused me to watch him fish, because he looked so like a big bear that you half expected him to dip a paw in the water and hook the fish out, instead of using a rod. It was getting so dark already, he was just a shape. I sat down beside him on the bank and trailed my hands in the water.

"How did it go?" he asked, and I told him. He must have known already; I couldn't have been the only one who came that way, but maybe he wanted to hear my version, being as I was the one who was supposed to make sure it went all right. I told it the way it happened, even down to how I'd warned Edo.

"I'm sorry it went wrong, Marti. Especially if it was because of what I did."

He sighed, and draped an arm round my shoulders. "No, I told him much the same thing, if he'd have listened. You can say "I told you so", if you want."

"Nothing I want less. I wish you'd been proved right. Did you see him after he left the yard?"

"No, he didn't come down here. He must have gone straight home. Do you think he'll come in tomorrow?"

"Jesus! I never even thought of it. No... never. I don't see how he could."

"I suppose not," he said thoughtfully, picking a grass stalk to chew, "but it would be better for him if he did." He took in his line and heaved himself up. "Maybe I'll call in and see him after supper."

"Good luck." I walked with him as far as his house door, and then back to mine. Suddenly all I wanted was to see Anni; find out if her backache was better; if she'd felt the baby kick and whether she'd had any company to listen to all day. I

101

thought of what must go through her mind sometimes, waiting to have the baby, wondering perhaps how much it would hurt and not able to ask anyone, and a wave of love and admiration swept over me.

I would find out if there was anything new she needed me to ask my mother or Hanna, or anything odd she fancied to eat. I would rub her back and arrange the cushions so she could rest better, and talk about anything she wanted me to.

I would even tell her about Edo, if she asked, which she would. It wouldn't make her happy, and maybe she would blame me more than Marti did, but I couldn't lie to her about it, because she trusted me.

16

HANNA

All through December, the house was full of singing. The Christmas service was coming close: Nico was in the boys' choir and Ria was due to sing too, and there didn't seem to be a moment one or other of them wasn't practising. Nico's voice had such a clear, fragile tone, it made me think of glass, and Ria's had strengthened a lot over the last six months or so. She sang whatever she was doing; it was almost like having Anni back home.

Poor Stevi must have felt a bit left out, being the only one who didn't sing. He takes after Marti in so many ways. He was trying to read the paper, with Nico piping across the room and Ria's voice floating in from the kitchen, and then we heard a couple of tom-cats outside, calling after our poor old tabby.

He threw down the newspaper. "Bloody hell, even the damn cats are at it!" He flung open the window and yelled: "Wrong place, wrong time. St Peter's, two weeks from now. You don't need to practise any more; you're perfect."

"Language..." I said, but I couldn't help laughing. "Anyway, shouldn't you be reading your schoolbooks, not the paper? I'm sure you must have holiday work."

"Oh, give it a rest, Mum. I'll get it done before we go back. The night before, probably."

"Oh, Stevi...."

"You should see the jobs in here. There's a load of work about, you know, and I could do it. You can get a start in most trades at the moment."

"But in any trade, you'll still have to learn, just like in school."

"No, not just like; I'd be *doing* something at the same time. I could handle that."

"And you'd have to move to town...."

"Well, I'd stay and work in the yard, if Dad would let me. Have another go at him for me?"

"It's a horrible place to work, you know. He wants better for you. For you to go to college; have the chance he didn't."

"What about what I want? Ask him? *Please?*"

"I'll see.... Not tonight; he's got other things to think about. When it's a good moment."

One more difficult subject to bring up, I thought as I got the supper ready to the sound of *When Adam was in Paradise*. I love those old carols. But I wasn't in quite the mood for them, and when I heard Marti at the door, and Andras with him, it didn't make me as happy as it normally would.

Andras knew as soon as I said hello that something wasn't right. He was getting very sensitive to tones of voice, and the things people said with their faces and bodies; he'd end up being as quick as Marti.

"It's all right, Andras, there's nothing wrong at your house. We've got something to tell you, but it'll wait. Have some coffee and rest a while."

He sat, looking a bit puzzled, but smiling as he listened to Nico and Ria, still trying to outdo each other. "Anni's going to enjoy hearing them in church, come Christmas. I'm really looking forward to taking her out of the house, and her seeing everyone for once. I can't wait to see her face when she steps through the front door."

I brushed the dust from Marti's jacket. "How was work?"

"Busy."

"How's that new lad doing, that Edo?"

"Well, he's still with us. Not bad at his work, from what I can see. How's he get on with the others, Andras?"

"He asks them for things he needs and passes them things when he has to. That's about the sum of it, really."

I felt a pang for him. I'd hoped he would be happier, away from his father.

"Is he lonely?" I asked.

Andras shrugged. "If he is, I'd be the last person he'd tell; he avoids me more than anyone."

I couldn't think why, unless Anni'd been wrong about the way he felt, and he was jealous of Andras. So I let it drop, and called Ria. Andras watched as she took a plate of soup upstairs.

"Isn't Bapa coming down to supper, then?"

"No, he isn't feeling too well today." I saw the cloud pass over his face as he realised he'd have to tell Anni that. I looked at Marti and he gave a little nod.

"Andras, love, that's what we need to tell you about. He isn't well at all; he hasn't been fit to come downstairs for some time now."

"How long is some time?"

"Since Gina was here... over a month."

"Nearer two. You never told me. Whenever I've asked after him, he'd just this minute gone up for a sleep."

"We were hoping he'd get better. We didn't want Anni to worry about him, in her condition, if we could avoid it."

"I'm not in that condition."

"Yes, but..." I looked at Marti for help, and he said: "You can't lie to her: we all know that. If she asked after him, and you knew he was ill, you'd have hellish trouble saying anything else. We didn't want to burden you with that." He's got such a deep growl of a voice; it always amazes me that it can sound so gentle on times.

"So why now?"

"Because..." Marti faltered, and I took it up. "Because it doesn't look as if he is going to get better. At least, the doctor's warned us not to hope for too much. We all hope that's wrong, but even if it is, God willing, he can hardly improve much in two weeks, in time for the Christmas service."

"When Anni goes out for the first time." His voice sounded dead, and I felt so sorry; it should have been such a happy time for them.

"He keeps saying he'll be there; it doesn't seem likely, but he's so stubborn, you can never tell. But if he isn't there, she'll know he can only be ill, and if he is there, she'll know when she sees him. So we need you to tell her, beforehand, so she'll be prepared."

"Oh, yes. Dead simple." He ran a hand through his hair; he looked desperate.

"I know you must hate bringing her any bad news, just now. But as long as you do it gently, it won't harm her; it's much safer than letting her find out suddenly."

He shook his head and rumpled his hair again. "You don't get it, do you? If I tell her now that he's been ill for weeks, why should she believe I haven't been lying to her? She's going to think I knew. I've never even kept anything from her unless I couldn't see what else to do, and I've never lied to her, not about anything."

Marti put a hand on his arm. "We'll make sure she knows that. I promise you, we'll let her know we kept it from you. If she's going to be upset with anyone, it can be us, not you."

"Oh, God, I can just hear it. *All those times you've been round there; you never saw him? In weeks? They told you he was all right? How curious were you, exactly?* You can get me out of that one too, can you? Because it's true. I hardly ever gave it a second thought." He sank his head in his hands. "She's going to hate me."

"Andras, love, all those weeks you had your mind full of her and the baby; it's perfectly natural. She'll understand that; she's probably feeling the same. Has she asked after him – after any of us – as much, since she was expecting?"

"She didn't think she had to; she thought she could trust me to keep my eyes open to what went on and tell her about it." He raised his head from his hands and said: "Can I see him?"

"Now? Well, I suppose so. I don't know what sort of a mood he's in, though. He has trouble breathing, and it makes him short-tempered at times."

"He's got every right to be. She'll ask me how he looks, and I ought to be able to tell her. I owe her that."

I took him upstairs to the old man's room: Marti came too. Ria was feeding him soup; he was trying to eat, but it can't have been easy; you could hear the rasp in his throat. He shook his head, and she moved the bowl away and wiped his lips.

Marti sat down by the bed and took his hand, holding it like a bird's egg. He stroked and kissed it, looking all the time into the old man's eyes. They looked milky, fixed on distance.

Andras hesitated a bit, but then he came to the other side, knelt by the bed and kissed his other hand.

The old man glanced at him, and his eyes seemed to clear. You could see the question in them. Andras understood. He spoke slow and clear, not too loud, looking straight into the old man's eyes, just as Anni always did. It's difficult for some folk to do that; they get embarrassed and drop their gaze – in fact, he always used to. But this time he never faltered.

"Anni is well. She sends her love." The old man didn't look sure of the last bit, so he tried again. "She says she loves you." That got through, and brought a smile. I could see the old man was trying to speak, and my heart was in my mouth because you could see it hurt him so much. But he was determined; he took his time, and had to stop mid-sentence with a searing cough, but he got it out.

"I'll see her. In church. At the.... Christmas... service." I felt concerned, and Marti gave a little despairing shake of the head, but Ria grinned and said: "That's right, Bapa; you tell 'em." I don't know how many of the words got through, but he understood her face very well and gave back the grin; she always seemed to put spirit in him. He gripped Andras's hand tighter, fixing him with his eyes like a hawk. "You... tell... her."

Andras nodded. He had to force himself, but he looked the old man in the eyes and spoke again: "I will tell her." The old man raised a hand, with difficulty, to Andras's head, and Andras bowed under it, right down to the counterpane.

I could see it was beginning to distress him, and the old man would be tiring himself too, so I got us out of the room. Marti stayed behind, still holding his hand; they were like that for hours sometimes.

Downstairs, I said: "I wouldn't get Anni's hopes up about seeing him at Christmas. I really can't see him making it to church."

"Oh yes he will," said Ria, "bet you what you like. If he says he's going, he'll be there. He's got more strength than any of you think, and enough guts for an army."

"He's worth an awful lot of me, that's for dead sure," said Andras, very quietly. Ria glanced at him, and said: "No, you're all right, you." I was surprised; it was the first really friendly thing she'd said to him in ages. I suppose it surprised him too; at any rate he looked very choked up for a minute or two, and by the time he had control of himself again, Ria was back sparring with Stevi. That young Karl who'd been showing an interest in her was hanging about outside, and Stevi was trying to tease her about him, complaining the tomcats were round again. But he couldn't get a rise out of her at all; Anni used to be much easier to tease about Andras.

"Do you think she might be right about him making it?" Andras asked me on the doorstep.

"I don't know. I think she sees what she wants to see; she doesn't want to know how ill he is. But he *is* a stubborn man, there's no doubt of that, and I know seeing Anni again means a lot to him. Let's just hope for the best."

Andras nodded. I said goodbye and wished him luck with telling Anni. "And from Marti too. I know he's thinking of you both as much as I am, but he's so much taken up with the old man just now."

"Yes," he said. He stood a moment, as if in thought, and added: "I really envy him."

17

ANDRAS; ANNI

Christmas morning was so bright. There was a bit of a gap in the curtains, and the light striking through it woke me early. I lay for a while, looking at Anni asleep, and experimented with putting a hand outside the covers and feeling how cold it was. I could hear my mother moving around downstairs already.

I reached out to the chair, for the clothes I'd taken off last night, and put most of them on under the covers. I'd have to get dressed in my good stuff to go to church, but right now I was just interested in keeping the cold out. I took a deep breath and slid out of bed. The floor was freezing – I hadn't been able to find last night's socks. I tiptoed over to the fireplace, riddled the ash a bit and got things going again. Then I went to the window. When I opened the curtains the light was almost painfully bright, and there were bluish-white frost-flowers on the glass.

Anni stirred, and woke. I came back to the bed and kissed her. "Happy Christmas."

She was still fuzzy with sleep. "Oh.... so it is. Same to you. What time is it?"

"Still early. Don't get up yet; wait till the room warms up a bit. I've got the fire going."

She reached out to the table by her side of the bed, picked up the locket I'd given her the night before, and opened it. It had some of my hair and hers in it. She smiled up at me and my heartbeat went all peculiar; she was so beautiful. Now the sickness had worn off, she seemed to glow from inside.

"What's the weather like?"

"Hard frost, by the look of it. You'll have to be dead careful out of doors."

"I can't believe I'm going to go out. Seven months, nearly..."

All the time she was getting ready, I could sense her excitement. She took ages plaiting her hair, as if it weren't all going to be hidden anyway, and when we went downstairs she could hardly eat – wouldn't have, if my mother hadn't made her. Knowing Bapa was ill had taken some of the shine off it; she was very worried about him, but even so, she couldn't help but be fired up. And it was just a walk through the village to the church, I thought; and wondered how I'd feel if that were a major event in my life.... When we stepped out of the front door, I swear I could feel her arm tingling.

I made her hold on to my arm all the way, because I was so scared she'd slip, but it wasn't as bad underfoot as I'd feared, and after a while I relaxed a bit and watched her enjoying it. The street, and the trees and bushes and everything, still glittered with frost, and her eyes sparkled. The sun caught her long silver coat, like it had on our wedding day, and I saw that it had faded a bit since then, though I'd never noticed before. And of course it didn't hang straight down, as it had then, but curved over her. And I'd thought the way she looked then was perfect, but now I liked this even better.

Everyone else was going the same way, and calling greetings to me and Mother and Auntie, and saying how well Anni looked. And I'd smile at her, and touch the scarf I was wearing, that she'd made me for Christmas. I felt dead happy. I wished I could talk to her, that was all. But sometimes I'd look at her and nearly speak, and I could see in her face that she knew what it was I'd have said.

Susi's face looks different. No, it's her hair; it's longer.... There's a plane tree been cut down, by the school; Andras didn't tell me about that. We used to climb that, when we were kids.

I can see snow up on the hills. Enough to sledge in, I reckon. They look so close. Half an hour, you can be at the top. You can see for miles from there. Over the fields and woods, a couple of towns in the distance. We used to point to some place and make up stories about it, and wonder if we'd ever go there.

Those girls laughing. Susi, Eva, Elli, Mags.... That was me, seven months ago. I'd have been in the middle of that, whatever it is they're whispering about. I don't feel so different. They're trying to make slides on the frosty pavement; it isn't icy enough but Andras steers me away anyhow, in case I fall.

It's a beautiful day: so still and glinting and the sound of people being happy. When we first came out I felt excited to be part of it again, but I'm not sure I am, now. When I saw the girls, I felt like running over to them, as if nothing had happened. As if I could just drop into the conversation. And I can't, any more than I can slide on the pavement or climb the hills. You can see there's nothing missing for them; it's like the space where I stood has closed up.

I hold on tighter, and Andras thinks I must be scared of falling and puts his arm around me.

The things I was feeling about her spilled over on to everyone else somehow; I couldn't see anyone without feeling friendly towards them. I even gave old Ossi a smile, and he was so surprised he made an attempt at one back. Edo didn't. Believe it or not, he was still in the yard every day; it must have taken some guts to come back, but it wasn't really working. The other lads resented him like hell, though they mostly left him alone, and he never made any attempt to change things. I'd made a couple of half-hearted efforts to be friendly, but he seemed to avoid me more than anyone; if he needed anything he'd ask Jos, who held him in contempt, or even Simo, rather than me. I didn't know why, and to be honest I didn't mind letting it be.

The holly bushes were absolutely covered, bright red with berries. I thought back to school, to the times I'd seen him with scratches all over his face, or his mouth bleeding. I'd tried then, too, sometimes, but never for long. Maybe if he'd been more forthcoming... but there was always this feeling about him: *Edo's weird; not quite right;* and the unspoken: *maybe you aren't either, if you hang around with him.*

He couldn't stop looking at Anni; of course it was the first time he'd seen her since the wedding and his eyes seemed to keep searching her face, as if he missed something. It crossed my mind that she might be mistaken, and that he did love her, and the thought made me feel such pity and kinship for him that I couldn't keep it out of my face; I wanted everyone to be happy, including him. But whatever he saw in my eyes, his stayed as expressionless as ever.

The choirboys had gone to church early, to practise, but by the time we got there, some of them had slipped the leash and were playing king-of-the-castle on the tombstones, in their white surplices – not so white now, some of them. I called Nico over, and he chatted while Anni cleaned a smear of mud off his face.

"Ria's in the church, with Mum. The others are on the way. Oh, hell...." The priest had come out, looking for the rest of his choir, and the way the cane twitched in his hand suggested he wasn't feeling festive. Nico dodged round me and shot into the church behind his back, while he was scolding the others.

I was still laughing when I felt Anni stiffen. I looked at her, and then followed her eyes. They were just coming through the gate: Marti and Stevi, and sure enough the old man was between them, leaning on them both. He was very pale, and you could see the cold air hurt his lungs; he was breathing shallow and carefully, and his eyes were staring with the effort. But when he saw her, he smiled, and then he shook off Marti and Stevi and started walking over to us. I could see Marti was in agony, dying to hold on to him, but he kept back, and the old man made it on his own, if a bit stiff and slow. She kissed him and hugged him as if she'd never let him go, and then made to help him into the church. But he shook his head, gesturing at her stomach, and gave her his arm. The pair of them had my heart in my mouth; I was glad when we were all sat down. Even then, she kept glancing across to him, and I doubt he ever took his eyes off her, except maybe when Ria was singing.

> When Adam he was all alone,
> A slumber it was granted him,
> A rib was taken from his side,
> To make up what was wanting....

I never knew she could sing like that. Well, she couldn't, half a year ago. Mum always said she'd have a good voice one day, but....

He looks so much older. His skin's like paper; you could almost see through it. But he's still hanging on; he won't let go till he's got no choice. Who would? He's still got a space to be in. But it's get-ting smaller. I can see now why it was so easy for them to keep it from Andras. People are getting used to him being asleep, on the edge of things, just not there.

I can sense Andras watching where my eyes are fixed, tensing in case I'm mad at him again. I reach for his hand. It was never him I was angry with, really. Or Mum and Dad, for that matter.

I wonder how much Bapa can hear. He's watching Ria, but I can't tell if he can hear the words. Her voice is a lot stronger than it was, but I reckon I've still got more volume, if I sang out.

I want you to see the baby. Please hang on. I'll sing to her, all the songs I know, and I'll give it all I've got so that you can hear too. Maybe he'll look like you. Does that make you feel better, knowing there'll be something of you still in the world, in Dad, in all of us? I don't know.

Nico looks like a little angel now; they all do, all those boys in white. Andras is smiling and shaking his head, thinking they aren't really like that at all. But he's wrong. For as long as they're here, singing this music, they're all they appear to be; they really do feel it. I know. When you sing in a group like that, in church or when the ballad-singer comes, something happens to you. When your voice becomes part of a bigger voice. There's a great freedom in it; you can really sing out, as loud and passionately as you want without fear, because if you do make a mistake it'll be lost in the wider sound. And sometimes you can let yourself go with it; feel your whole self swallowed up, floating away on the music....

Where is the kingly palace,
good man; please to say?
We come to see the little prince
who is born today.

For a while, there isn't a you or a them any more; what was you is part of all of you. And that gives you a great feeling, and yet it's scary too. It feels as if part of you could go beyond your body and live for ever. But it's like dying as well, because to do it you have to give up what's just you, the space where only you were. Even for a few moments, that's not easy.

There is no kingly palace,
sirs: there is no king.
We are a poor village,
and dream of no such thing.

*That's Nico, singing the solo response. He's heartwrenching. No
wonder they talk about boys' voices breaking; his is perfect now,
but it sounds as brittle as one of Auntie's eggs. Just another couple
of years, I suppose; then it's gone. Things ought to last longer.*

*Singing solo is scary too, but in a different way. In the silence,
you can really hear yourself being you and nobody else. If it goes
wrong, you're on your own, but when it works... oh, there was
nothing like it.*

*The priest's hand raises us now, to join in. It's hard to remem-
ber not to sing, not even softly behind the veil. No voice yet. But
I stand up with the rest. Andras looks as if he'd rather I didn't;
but I want to. Dad wishes Bapa wouldn't either, but he knows how
far arguing will get him. Our eyes are fixed on each other; it feels
as if I help him get up. Once he's standing, Dad puts an arm
around him and he leans back; you can see how much he needs it.
Dad's taking his whole weight as if it were nothing. But he stood
up on his own.*

*I know, Bapa; I know. I can still hear you being you. But I
don't know what me being me sounds like any more. I'm not sure
I remember what sound I used to make, and if I ever hear myself
again, it might not be the same. Maybe there isn't a me any more;
maybe your voice can really get lost, swallowed up in the music....*

I felt her sway against me, and my heart lurched. I knew standing up for the singing wasn't a good idea. But she wouldn't sit
down again; just shook her head and gestured towards her
folks, as if she didn't want to worry them. So I put my arm
round her, instead, and tried to support her all I could, so she
wouldn't feel she was standing alone.

18

BAPA

Just a couple of months to go. Maybe less. Know she's all right; see the baby. I can go on till then. I got out of bed today. First time since Christmas. Seven steps to the armchair by the window. I felt shaky, but that's with not having stood up for so long. It's been bad, all right, but maybe I've turned the corner now. Give it a few days, I might be able to get out and visit her. Hanna shakes her head when I suggest that; says it's still too cold out of doors, and with the snow underfoot.... *Wait till the weather changes.* Easy to say 'wait', when you're that age.

My window looks over the street. When she settled all the shawls round me, Hanna said it was a pity there wasn't more going on out there this time of year, for me to look at. She can't have been looking very hard, or she's got better things to do. It never stops out there.

Over the road, there's a little tree heavy with berries, and the way it's moving, you'd think there was a high wind. It's alive with birds, little brown ones, picking the berries, dropping them in the snow, squabbling over them. They must be making a hell of a racket. I wonder what kind they are. How did I get to be seventy-whatever-it-is, and never learn to tell one from another? I suppose I just never took a fancy to know, before. Or there wasn't time. Things to do. No, there would have been, if I'd wanted. Time, I mean. Think of all the time you waste.

Adam in the city, he says he can't find the time to come down here. Too much work; can't leave the business. He'd find it, if he wanted to. I don't blame him. I'd do things differently, if I had them to do again: I never got it right with him. Kati used to say we were too alike. *That's why you argue all the time; you're both too stubborn to back down.* Good, coming from her; she was just the same.... But it was true he and I set each other off somehow. God, we had some shouting-matches.

It was strange when he came back as a man, because that spark just wasn't there any more. We'd sit and chat; no tension, no annoyance, like a couple of polite strangers, which was what we'd become. My fault, but it hurt to think so. I'd make meaningless conversation and long for the days when we cared enough to scream at each other. I wonder if he missed them, too.

I can't quite see her house from here; the road bends too much. I saw Emmi in the street a while ago, blowing her fingers with the cold; she smiled and signed: "Anni's well". And young Andras comes up to see me nearly every day on his way home; I suppose she sends him to see how I am. I'm getting very fond of him, actually; there's a lot of kindness in him. I must be going soft.

The little birds seem to be fighting over something; I can't tell what it is. What's important enough, I want to ask them; don't you know you could be dead this time next year. But of course they don't, do they; birds?

Someone's come in; I feel the vibration in the floorboards. I turn my head, and it's young Ria, come to mend the fire. They keep it on all day in my room; it may be cold out, but you couldn't complain of lack of warmth in here. She gets the flames leaping again, and comes over to the window.

She speaks. The shapes look like: "Anything going on?" I shake my head. "Not much. Saw Stevi – must be dodging school. Don't tell your dad." She grins and nods. I *am* going soft. If I caught mine cutting school, I used to slap them, but it doesn't seem so important now. I show her the tree full of quarrelling birds, and she smiles. Another set of shapes; a long sentence this time. Concentrate. I can make out "Nico" and "choir", I think. I laugh, and shake my head: "You're wicked, you."

She's so like my Kati. I love Anni because she takes after Hanna; she makes everyone feel happy around her. A bit sparkier than Hanna, though. And Ria livens everyone up where she is; keeps them on their toes. But she's got more self-control than Kati ever had. I've seen her, often enough, grin and keep her thoughts to herself when Kati would have told the street.

I'm glad when she comes in; glad to talk and listen to her;

it makes me feel alive. But it's getting bloody difficult. Talking makes my throat ache like hell after a few words, and if I go on long enough it brings on the cough again, and that's like being kicked in the ribs by a horse. And watching people talk, trying to make out the shapes, takes more concentration than I've used since I gave up work. You can't keep it up for long; at least I can't.

So I cut things short; leave out words, or don't bother to mention things at all. And give up on the shapes, so that folk just sign what they want to say – or discover they didn't really need to say it. When Ria kisses me and goes back downstairs, part of me's sad, but part is glad of the rest. It feels so much easier sometimes, not to bother. There's a lot of talking and listening, now, that I wish I'd done while I still could.

Stevi looked as if he was heading for the river. That's risky, because it's so close to the tanyard, but then he's as keen on fishing as his dad.... Not the weather for it, but I suppose anything's better than school. With any luck, Marti'll be too busy to leave the yard, and if any of the lads get down there in their break, they won't tell on him. Marti did his share of sloping off to fish; Adam too, and I told them they'd come to a bad end, but they haven't yet. And Nicolas... all those years in school, for what? Bloody typhus didn't care if he could read or not – nor that he was kind and bright and good company. Twenty-two. I wish I'd told him to spend every day down the river, while he could.

I'm tired, but I don't want to sleep. I grudge every moment I spend asleep now. I want to keep looking out of the window; see everyone who passes, every twitching curtain, every bird that lights on the tree. I don't want to miss anything. Sleep's a waste of time.

I watch the women, going to and fro between each other's houses, or coming from the shop, deep in gossip, and I'd like to be listening over their shoulders – much good that would do me. I don't suppose they're talking about anything that matters; I just want to *know*.

The light's going already: winter days seem to last no time. *This time of year, night comes on horseback.* Who used to say that? Kati? Or it might have been my mother.

Short person with a long shadow coming down the street. Nico, home from school. Gives me a wave and a smile. He's always friendly, when I see him.

Stevi, coming from the wrong direction. I raise my eyebrows; he gives me a rueful grin and puts his hands together as if he's praying. I put my finger to my lips and nod, and he mouths: "Thanks", and something else I can't make out.

It used to be bedlam in this house, when they all got home from school: dogs barking hello and everyone talking at once. I'm sure it still is: no reason to suppose things stop happening just because you aren't part of them any more.

I can hardly see the street any more. But I know every stone of it. Every stone of every street in the village, not that there are many. And every path in the woods, and every way up the hills. When I was young, I used to think of travelling: well, that never happened. I've spent seventy-something years here, and you can get to know a place very well in that time.

When I could still get out, strangers would ask sometimes: "Have you lived here all your life?" I always said: "Not yet".

I want to see the baby. And I quite fancy another look at bluebells. And the smell of cut grass in the summer, and the taste of peaches....

The street's filling up with little groups of lads now, back from the yard. The young ones planning what they'll do tonight, and the married ones knowing. Dear God, how can Leo look so old?

One on his own; what is it with that Edo? Always watching from the edge of things. He gives me the creeps.

Lights are coming on in the houses, but most of the light in the street comes from the snow; blue and uncanny in the dusk. It makes things look different. Not the man walking towards the house now, though; I'd know him in any light, and not just because he's built the way he is.

He looks up at me; smiles; bows his head a little. He'll be up here soon, when he's said hello to Hanna and the children. He looks tired, but he doesn't stay as late at the yard as he used to, these days.

We always got on fine, when he was a lad – he could get on with anybody – but I used to think he was very unlike me. I'd look at him and wonder how a scrawny article like me could have made someone the size of him – he took after Kati's dad, I know, but it still seemed odd. And I'd watch him in an argument and marvel at how he kept his temper, when he could have flattened anyone with one hand. God help us, I got heated about something once, when he was about sixteen, and slapped him. That happened fairly often with Adam; never with him, because he never needed it; but that one time I did, and then almost at once I thought: *am I mad; he's twice my size.* And I stood back, wondering what he'd do, and I think I was really scared. But he just stood a moment, looking down at me, and then went about whatever he was doing; never a word... I nearly apologised.

When he comes in, he goes to light the lamp, but I say: "Not yet". I like the firelight. He gestures at the bed, and I nod – there's nothing left to see in the street now, and I'm tired. He moves all the shawls and things gently aside; I put my arms round his neck and he lifts me as if I were made of air. He carries me to the bed as easily as if his arms were empty, and sorts the pillows out with one hand while I rest in the crook of his other arm. When they're ready, he makes to move his arm out from behind me, but I huddle against him a bit, and he leaves it there.

Ever since I started to go deaf, I've found his voice harder to understand than any other, because it's so deep and echoing. It used to grieve him, I think, but now he's just about given up trying to get through that way, we do much better. He doesn't bother signing much, either. He'll sit here for ages with his arms round me, or his hand in mine, or stroking my hair. I've gone to sleep on his shoulder, and woken hours later to find him asleep too.

I remember when he was first born – my first – and I'd hold him like that, and think: *I couldn't have made anything that perfect,* and tell him I loved him. And then when they get a bit bigger, you're never quite as close as that again, certainly not with boys anyhow, and not with words. I can't see either of us coming out with: "I love you", that's for sure. But when I rest on his arm, I feel myself shake with love. I expect he takes it for a tremor. Damn well hope so, anyway.

I don't know if I've always loved him this much, and just never realised till now. Same with bluebells and the scent of grass. And Hanna and the children and young Andras and this baby I might never see. I know one thing. They let you spend all your life getting fond of people and places and things, getting attached to them by a hundred little hooks, like ivy to the cracks on a wall, and then they say: *Pull yourself free; tear yourself away; leave them all behind.* Call that fair? I bloody don't.

19

ANDRAS

I remember noticing the crocuses that morning. I never used to pay any mind to flowers; left all that to my mother, until Anni got so keen on them. There was still snow on the ground, and the green and gold of the early crocuses was so bright and piercing against it.

I didn't meet Marti on the way to work, but then he often got in early if he had paperwork to sort. Or I might have been a bit later than usual. Anni was so dreamy and slow in the mornings now, and I caught the mood from her; some days I could hardly get out of bed.

I glanced in the site office as I passed, expecting to see him at his desk, but there was little wizened Leo, looking like an empty space by comparison. He beckoned me into the office.

"Boss sent to say he won't be in. Family. His old man passed on last night. He wants you to call round."

I sat down. I couldn't say anything for a moment. Leo looked surprised.

"Hardly unexpected, was it? He looked on the way out, last time I saw him."

"He won't see the baby," I said. "I wish he'd lived for that."

"Well, then he'd have wanted to be spared for summer, and then Christmas... There's never a right time to go, lad, so it's just as well we don't get asked."

"I've got some hides need shifting... I'd better see Jos."

"No, it's all right. I know where everything's at. The boss keeps good records, give him that." He waved a pen at Marti's neat lists and charts. "The sooner he's back keeping them, the better. I can't be doing with this."

He held the pen like a shovel. I thought how deft he was with the wicked craft knives, how thin he could shave a hide. He must have been thinking something the same.

"Marti's old man used to be a beamsman too, you know. He

taught me."

"I never knew that." I'd never known, either, that Leo was that much younger than Bapa; I'd always thought of him as ancient and it came as a shock that he was only around Marti's age.

"No, well, he hasn't been exactly talkative for years. I mean hadn't. Do I? Hasn't; hadn't?" Words weren't Leo's speciality.

I knew I couldn't leave it long. Marti would want me to tell Anni before someone like Auntie picked it up on the street. But I took a walk round the yard first, trying to sort my thoughts out. Anni'd never told me what he used to do for a living, but then I'd never asked. I never thought of him at work; he was the old man, who sat by the fire or in the sun waiting for people to remember he was there. As long as I'd known him, he'd had a tremor in his hands; it seemed incredible to think of him using those knives. And yet he had; he'd been a workman, and a lover, and a husband and father; he'd stood in all the places I had. And now... When I first heard, I'd thought only of her and how she'd feel. I hadn't really ever been that close to him, yet now I felt as if a bit of me had gone.

Jos came over. "Sorry about the old man, mate. Hope she doesn't take it too hard. We're all thinking of her."

"She will, but thanks anyway. I'll tell her. Hey, any sign of Edo today?"

Jos snorted. "No. That's three days the useless bastard's been missing; I hope the boss isn't planning to put up with it much longer."

Ria let me in to the house. Her hair was covered, in mourning, and it made her look more like Anni than I'd ever seen her. So did her grief. I thought of what folk said about her, that she always had an answer ready. She didn't for this, and she looked helpless. I hugged her and Hanna, and said something to the boys. They looked downcast, but not in quite the same way as Ria and Hanna, and I guessed there was some guilt mixed up in it for them. They hadn't really spared him much time lately, but you couldn't be too hard on them for that, at their age. God knows, I was old enough to have done better, and I hadn't.

Marti had been sorting things in his father's room, but when he heard me he came down, carrying a box that looked the size of a tea-chest. He looked pale and rumpled, as if he hadn't slept. Hanna and Ria disappeared to the kitchen, cooking for the wake, I suppose, and the lads sat around looking awkward until Marti said gently: "Go out for a walk or something; he wouldn't mind."

They were off like rabbits out of a trap; only decency kept them from running. Marti glanced through the window at them and sighed. His eyes were red. Nothing could have been more natural, yet it shocked me a bit, as if I'd seen my father cry. I stretched out a hand to him, and he crushed it in both his.

"How is she?"

"Fine... at least, she was this morning."

"You'll have to tell her. It shouldn't come as too much of a shock, after the way he was at Christmas.... Tell her it was peaceful; he died in his sleep."

I nearly asked if that was true, and then realised I didn't want to know. I said nothing. I should have been trying to comfort Marti, but instead it was he who said to me: "He died knowing the baby was on the way; he was happy about that. And he managed to get out and see her that last time, as he wanted."

It was much the sort of thing I'd been planning to say to Anni, but hearing it from someone else suddenly snapped my patience.

"He should have been able to *speak* to her! Hear her voice. He was miserable without her. And she worried about him, and missed him, and.... oh, this whole custom stinks, Marti, it's cruel and it's pointless; it's made her unhappy and it probably helped kill him.... oh, Marti, I'm sorry..." His hand had clenched involuntarily on mine, and the pain made me think what I was saying. It was lucky it was my left hand, because I couldn't use it properly for two days.

"I shouldn't have said that. But I mean it about this daft business. They've all but got rid of it in the city and the big towns, why are we still putting up with it here?"

123

"I don't see it lasting much longer. Your children will read about it and laugh."

"Like hell they will. I'll tell them how much pain it caused, and for no good reason on earth."

"How will Anni feel about that, I wonder? Or your mother, or Hanna? How will you feel, if twenty years hence they find some brilliant new way of getting tannin and your son falls about laughing at the thought of you doing your throat in, grinding bark?"

"I'll be glad *he* doesn't have to, for a start. And it isn't the same, Marti, you know it's not. The bark's needed; this isn't. What possible good does it do?"

His tired face creased into a very slight, momentary smile. "Hanna asked me the very same question, the other day."

"I'm not surprised."

"She was talking about the yard ritual, the one poor Edo flunked. She got most indignant; said it was cruel and pointless and I should put a stop to it."

"Well, maybe she's right."

"You don't really think that."

"All right, I don't. But I could be wrong. And anyway you can't compare the two. An hour or so against years?"

"No," he agreed, "you can't. It's just interesting what makes different people indignant... Did you know it was women who clung on to it longest in the city? Look, if Ria and my granddaughters never go through it, I'll be well pleased. I hope it does come to an end. But anything that lasts a while generally does *something* that people want." He opened the box, took out some things wrapped in paper and put them carefully on the table. As he unwrapped them, I saw they were stones, eggs, dried flowers. They were all blue.

"My mother's," he said quietly, "all presents from him. She kept them all, every one, and then after she died, he did.... Being everything to each other... maybe you could still do it without the old way, but who knows? They had that: I've had it. So did your mother and father, if you could only remember. I want it for my children too. I want what you told me about lying awake at night, worrying about her, feeling responsible for her happiness, impatient for her voice. I did all that too. And I want it for Anni."

"I could still do all that, without her going through this." My voice was a bit shaky. "And what about the ones it goes wrong for? What sort of a life would any wife of Simo's have?"

"A miserable one under any system, I should think. There's always someone. The business in the yard didn't work for Edo either, but it does for most."

"You can talk all you want, Marti: you argue better than I do. But I hate what's happening to Anni, and I'll never believe you don't. It isn't fair, and it isn't sense."

"No, it isn't; and it'll have to change. I don't think you can force the pace, though. And you might have to leave *something*, if it's got the same meaning for women as the yard ritual has for the lads.... By the way, I heard something yesterday; did you know Edo's gone to live in the city?"

"No? All on his own? He's got more guts than I have, then; that'd terrify me."

"Different folk, different fears." Marti gave a huge yawn. He picked up one of the little blue stones and said: "I'm not a son any more. It feels rather odd."

"It feels odd knowing I'm going to be a father. I can't get used to it."

"*You* can't get used to it; how about me; you're turning me into a grandfather.... I wonder what name your eldest will invent for me? I'm not sure I could cope with Bapa."

He took a big, worn, flattish case out of the box. "Look at these."

I opened it. It was a set of craft knives, like Leo's. They were all there, the blunt, two-handled unhairing knife, the double-edged flesher with its concave and convex blades, the triangular-bladed striking pin and the butcher's knife with its vicious edge, keen enough for the finest hairs.... They were all clean, all beautifully polished as if they might be needed any minute.

"I reckon he must have cleaned them every day," Marti said softly. I was choked up; I just couldn't answer. I felt I was looking at a man in a box. All those times I'd watched him across a table, or from the side of a bed, so on the edge of things, so distant, as if most of him weren't there at all. Where *had* he been; wrapped up in paper with blue memories; in this case where he kept his working life? There suddenly seemed to have been several of him, and I'd only ever known the one, if that.

"I used to hope Stevi would fancy going to college," said Marti, "after all, that was partly why I was making the money in the first place... But he shows no inclination; he'd sooner be in the yard than in school. He's the practical sort; very like the old man, really." (And you, I thought, but I kept it to myself.)

Marti ran his finger idly along the blade of the fleshing knife, while I clenched my teeth; he was using the blunter, concave, side, but it still put me on edge. "I think," he said, "I'll ask Leo if he fancies having an apprentice. Tell her that, too."

I was still staring at the knives. Marti tilted my face up and asked: "What's the matter?"

It was hard to tell him, because I wasn't sure. I'd had a sort of vision, as he was speaking, of him turning into Bapa, and Stevi into him, and then the baby was born and it turned into me, but what I turned into was an empty space.

"I don't know how to be a father. I might turn out to be one like Ossi."

"I can promise you there's no chance of that happening."

"How?"

"Because I'd come after you with these. I'd be in the queue behind Anni and Hanna and your mother, though."

He hugged me, and I thought: why was I worrying about a mere hand; here go the ribs....

"Your dad was a good man, Andras, and a good husband and father. She must miss him a lot, still. I suppose that's why she doesn't talk about him. But she owes you him; the picture in her mind, the shape he made in the world. Everyone needs that. Go home now, and as soon as Anni can spare you, go and tell your mother you need to know him."

20

EMMI

I slipped out after dinner, while the lass was having a sleep. I don't like leaving her alone for long, so close to her time, but she generally sleeps for an hour or so in the afternoon, these days.

There weren't many in the churchyard; just a few relatives freshening flowers and old Jacob, tidying the grass. He gave me a nod as I passed; we're such old acquaintances, we have hardly anything left to say.

I took out last week's crocuses and tipped the stale water out on the grass. It never gets brown by this stone, even in a hot summer. I refilled the pot from the water butt by the church wall, and took it back to the stone.

Hello Jon. I've brought a few narcissus. The crocuses and snowdrops are just about dead now, and there isn't much else about yet, but these came out yesterday and I thought you'd like them. I took half into the house, to cheer the lass up, and brought the rest here.

It's another rainy day. I wonder why this weather brings the weeds on, when it does nothing for the flowers? There's so much I should be doing in the garden... as soon as the sun comes out, I must clear some of the old growth away, before it chokes the spring bulbs.

Well, you should be a grandfather soon. Everything's going as it ought to. She seems to be getting over the old man's death now; we haven't had any more crying fits for a couple of weeks. I suppose, all in all, she took it better than she might have done – even last month, when she was really miserable, she forced herself to eat, for the baby. I remember how it does that to you; you can't really care about anything else. I know, when I was that far gone with Andras, the whole village could have been struck by lightning; I don't think I would have noticed. Except for you, of course.

When Andras comes in, she lights up from inside; it's like being alive in a different way. And he's the same about her. Sometimes we'll be talking, and I can feel his mind just wander off when he looks at her. At least they can eat supper now. When they first married, they hardly bothered; they were too desperate to get away on their own. Remember us? And you think you're close then, but you're wrong. Close is when it gets so that you can wait for that, because you're sure of it. When you can talk without words, because you know what they'd be. When he's just as much yours on the other side of the room, or at work, or down the pub for the evening, or away on business, or lying under a stone.

Not that you don't worry. Andras is terrified, the closer she gets, in case it goes wrong and he loses her. He won't go out with the lads much now, and if he does, he's home early. He's stopped working all hours at the yard too, I've noticed; it's as if he wants to spend all the time he can with her. And I've seen her look at your photograph and at me, when she thinks I'm not watching, and you can see it in her eyes: *if that happened to Andras, I couldn't go on.*

Well, I thought I couldn't, of course, but the sun would keep rising and setting just as usual, and there was Andras to think of. During the day I told myself you were at work, and in the evening you were out with the lads, and at night you'd had to go on a trip, but you'd be back next day for sure. And I kept on talking to you in my head, same as I'd always done when you weren't there or we couldn't speak. I got really quite good at holding two conversations at once.

And you always had plenty to say, because I told you all the news; kept you up to date with everything. I wouldn't let things go on without you. I brought up Andras, and kept the house going, and did what handwork I could to bring a bit more in besides what your folk gave me, and everyone said how well I was coping without you. But I could never have done that.

Look, you might as well know. Andras came to me the other day and asked me to talk about you. He said I never had, and I suppose it's true. I've always hated saying your name and the word *was*. He *was... Jon was...* as long as I don't say *was*, I can think *is*.

But he said he needed to; that he couldn't be a father if he didn't have one. And I said: but you did; for three years you had as loving a father as anyone could want. And he looked unhappy and said: "I can't see him, Mum. I've tried and tried, and I can't see him or hear him in my head."

I couldn't help feeling guilty, thinking how I hear you in my head every day; see you, almost, if I turn round a bit quick. I should have shared you with him. But when he was younger, it didn't seem to matter. We were so close, and he seemed happy, and I'd hear folk say: *she's everything to him, father and mother both....* Maybe I didn't want to share him with you, either.

Anyway I'm sorry if I got it wrong. Who's perfect? I told him what you were like around the house, and how you pulled up all the lilies before they flowered, because you thought they were weeds, and how you were with him. He wanted to know about all the things you did with him; the games you played and the daft names you called him, and everything we did together. It was strange: I thought even I must have forgotten most of that, but it comes back if you try. And just now and then, I'd recall a silly word you'd invented, or some toy you'd made him, and it'd spark something; he'd light up and say: "I remember that!"

After you... weren't there, I never much liked people saying Andras was the image of you. He wasn't, anyway; I've always seen both of us in him, but I didn't *want* there ever to be another one of you. I think that's why I've been hoping for a grand-daughter, because if it's a boy they'll surely call him Jon. Even more so now, because it was Anni's grandfather's name, too.

But I think I could live with it now. It's going to be very odd, watching him stand in your place and a new baby in his. I can't see you with grey hair and an old face: I can't fit *that* you into things at all. You're still a young man, a young father, and soon he's going to be... not you, exactly, but where you were. And where'll you be? If there were any justice, you'd have moved on, like me. But you didn't. And now there'll be no place for you, unless it's in things Andras does and says, or the baby's face.

Jon, but not the same Jon. My Jon, but Anni's grandfather too. And me, and Andras, and Hanna and all of us. Just odd little bits, here and there, so that you see some action or hear a turn of phrase and think: *why, that's him to the life.*

Do you recall the place in the bluebell wood, where that little peat burn runs into the river? You should.... It's a golden brown, that burn, and it runs into the clear river like a vein; you can see the thread of brown for a long way. And if the water isn't so clear lower down, it's because so many veins have run into it and coloured it different; made it something more than it was before. It'll get to the sea, and the burn will still be there, even if folk can't see it any more; it'll still have made the journey.

I must go; she'll be awake soon. I'll come next week as usual, provided we aren't in the middle of having the baby. Put in a good word for us up there, if anyone's listening.

As I turned to go, I saw someone standing by the newest grave, and for a second I couldn't think who, but then I saw it was young Ria. She still had her hair covered, and it made her face look a lot more like Anni's – they weren't much alike normally, especially the hair. Ria took after Hanna in looks, though in character she reminded me much more of Marti's mother, old Kati. Which was odd if you like, because there weren't two women on the face of the earth more unlike than Hanna and Kati.... But there, it's as I was saying to Jon; no-one ever gets made twice.

I waited at the gate, and she caught up.

"How's Anni?"

"Fine. Not long to wait now." She nodded, but she didn't look happy.

"She'll be all right. That sort of thing runs in families. Your mother had four with no trouble; you and Anni will be the same."

She winced. "I'm not sure I fancy all that."

"Well now, the way you and young Karl have been looking at each other since last autumn, I thought you might."

"He does the looking – most of it, anyway."

"You're not that gone on him, then?"

She hesitated. "I like him. I could like him more, maybe."

"If?"

"If I didn't keep thinking what can happen when you like someone. He might die. Or I might, if I had a baby. Or it might go wrong, like it has for Uncle Adam."

"Oh, is *that* why she didn't come down to the funeral with him? She should have done it for manners, though.... Hanna's never said a word about this."

"I probably wasn't supposed to say either; I think Mum's a bit embarrassed about it. But they're living apart, and Gina says in her letters her mother's fearfully unhappy."

"Mm. Well, it doesn't come with a guarantee, that's for sure. But what else are you going to do? You can't *stop* yourself loving someone just because you might lose them. And if you could, who would you start with – your father, your mother? Are you sorry you loved your grandfather?"

She twisted a handkerchief in her hand. "A bit, at the moment... no, I don't mean that. But I don't feel like any more grief yet."

We walked on without words for a while, before she spoke again.

"Tell you one thing I'm not doing; I'm not going through this silence business. If Karl wants me, he can have me without that. Gina was right about it, you know."

"Didn't notice you backing her up at the time."

"Yes, well, she shouldn't have been fluttering her eyelashes at Andras. She always had a thing for him... But she's right about that."

"Maybe. It does seem to be dying out."

"You must be sorry it didn't die out in time for you."

"What's the point of regretting anything? It happened: I became one person instead of another."

"It won't happen to me."

"What will you do; move to town?"

"Not if I can help it. I'd rather find someone who's prepared to stay here and just not do it. I want it both ways, and I reckon you can have it, if you don't let anyone tell you different."

"Well, I wish you luck with it, truly. I hope you can."

She paused outside her door. "Kiss Anni for me."

"You could come and do that."

She shook her head. "After. I'm too scared for her, and it might show. I don't want to upset her."

Back home, the lass had woken up and started to get things ready for Andras. I shook my head, but I didn't stop her helping, just tried to make sure she didn't overdo it. She liked to keep busy; it took her mind off things.

The clock chimed, and she smiled all over her face, because she knew he'd soon be in. I looked across at Auntie, reading about whatever folk were doing in town, which filled up a fair amount of her day, and I thought: I really do hope Ria gets what she wants... but if there had to be a choice, I'd sooner be someone with a reason to watch the clock.

When he came in, she started over to him, but he stopped that and made her sit down and sorted the cushions round her, so her back wouldn't ache so much. And then when he straightened up he had to shake the hair back out of his eyes....

At suppertime he was talking about Marti and Hanna, and I asked: "Have they got any kittens over there just now?"

"Eh? Yes; when haven't they? Why do you ask?"

"I thought it might be nice to have a cat."

"Wouldn't it damage the flowers?"

"Well, I expect you can train them. And they're good company."

He looked across at her, and smiled at the way her eyes sparkled at the thought of it.

"Are you sure? What about the goldfish?"

"Oh, put some net over the pond or something. There has to be a way to have the best of both worlds."

21

ANNI

When I first woke, I just felt restless, and I shifted around trying to get comfortable. But I couldn't, so I slipped out of bed without waking Andras and walked around the room, trying not to step on any creaky boards. I still had these twinges, but it felt better than lying down.

Then I had something that felt like a definite pain, and I wondered if this was it. But I knew you could have false alarms. Emmi and Mum had talked about it, and I thought: I'll feel such a fool if I wake everyone and nothing happens. And the pain soon went away. After a while, I realised I should have noted the time, in case there was another one, but I hadn't.

I got tired after a while, but I still didn't fancy lying down, so I went over and sat by the window. I drew the curtain back; it was the dead of night still, so there was no danger of any light waking him. It was a clear, cold night and all the stars were out. I hadn't seen that for ages. When we were first married, Andras and I would sit up in the starlight sometimes, because we didn't want to stop talking and go to sleep, but we weren't looking at the stars much. I'd rather have looked at his face any time.

They were very beautiful, though. I sat there and thought: Uncle Adam can see these in the city; poor Edo too, now. That ballad-singer, wherever he is; they're the same for him. All over the country; all over the world. I wondered if Bapa could see them, and whether they looked the same for him.

The pain came back. It took me by surprise and I made a bit of a noise, but he didn't wake. I tried to think how long since the last one, but I was only guessing. I looked at the clock and thought: I'll give it one more; then I'll know exactly how long. And you never know, it might go away...

I suppose I knew it wouldn't; that it wasn't a false alarm. But though I'd waited so long, I wished now I could stop it. I wanted it to be over; I just didn't want it to happen. Or I didn't want to

be awake while it happened. Yes I do. In case something goes
wrong. I have to say goodbye. It was getting cold by the window.
I shivered, looking into the dark and trying to make out shapes in
the garden – the pond, the magnolia tree. Its pale candles had just
started to come out, and for some daft reason I suddenly wanted to
see them, even vaguely in the night. I strained my eyes, wondering
if the dark was a bit paler at some points, but I couldn't decide. I
don't know why it mattered, but it did, and I was on the edge of
crying.

Then I looked back at our bed, and I saw a dark stain where
I'd been lying. It was blood; it must have happened while I was
asleep. It's... what did they call it? A show. It's all right; it's meant
to happen. But it means it's started, doesn't it? How long ago?

I remembered why I liked his face better than stars.

"Andras. Andras, wake up." *He stirred and muttered, and*
then he seemed to snap awake in a second.

"Christ! What is it? Has it started?"

"I think so. Can you wake Emmi?"

"Yeah... yes, of course. Will you be all right while I'm
gone?"

"What, across the landing? Get on with it!"

But even in the few minutes he was gone, I did get scared. I looked
at the stars again, and thought: I wish I'd taken more notice of them;
they're so beautiful and I don't even know which is which.

Just as Andras got back with Emmi, I had another pain. I showed
Emmi where, and she had a look at me and changed the sheet, and
asked Andras: "How long since the last one?" *He didn't know, of*
course, but I signed: About fifteen minutes.

Emmi nodded, and turned back to him. "That's all right, then.
I'll go and make some tea."

He churned his fingers through his hair. "Isn't anything happening, then?"

"Oh, it's on the way, all right, but nothing much is going to
happen for a long while yet. You and Anni can sit and chat
and have a cup of tea; I'll get some things ready."

"Shouldn't she be in bed?"

"Not if she's easier out of it. What would you know, anyway?

When the next pain comes, hold her and check the time."

When she brought the tea, she squeezed my hand and smiled, but then she went out again so that Andras and I could talk. We could hear her downstairs, moving softly about; after a while we heard low voices so we knew Auntie was up too. Andras got the fire started. I hadn't realised how cold I'd become, until I started getting warm again.

"Andras, do you know the names of the stars?"

"Eh? No; can't say I do. Maybe someone told me in school once, but it's one of those things that don't stay in your head, unless you need to know."

"There's so many things. Places you don't go to, and things you don't do. I wonder how many songs there are, that I've never heard."

"Hey, there's loads of time yet. What is it; are you scared?"

"Yes."

"So am I."

I laughed, because here he was meant to be reassuring me, and he was just as bad.... And in the middle of the laugh the pain came again, worse this time.

"All right... it's all right... hold on to me."

"Time... check the clock..."

"There. There, love. All right? Good. Twelve minutes."

He called down the stairs to tell Emmi, and she came up and had another look at me. I tried to return her smile, but I wasn't feeling very brave. She stood for a moment looking down at me, then turned to Andras.

"Go down the road and wake Hanna. Don't panic; there's still plenty of time. Just tell her everything's going well but Anni could do with her here."

"Should I get Greta as well?"

"Oh, no need of that as long as everything's all right. She's close enough, if we need her later. Just bring Hanna back."

He went down the stairs two at a time, and Emmi raised her eyes to heaven and shook her head. I signed "thanks" and she stroked my hair and held my hand while we waited. The pain came again, and she held me through it and checked the clock. I looked "is it all right?" at her, and she smiled and nodded, and held me again until we heard the front door open.

I heard a voice downstairs which could only be Dad's, and then Mum's tread on the stairs, and she came in and kissed me.

"How often?"

"About ten minutes apart and getting less. She had one five minutes ago."

Dad's face appeared round the door. He waved at me and said to Mum: "Shouldn't she be in bed?"

Andras was right behind him, looking worried: "I still reckon I should fetch the midwife, Mum."

"Experts. We seem to be surrounded by them. Go away." *Dad grinned, waved again and went downstairs, but I held on to Andras's hand. Mum patted his shoulder.*

"She's close enough if we need help, love. I've had four, remember, and I helped my sisters with theirs. Everything's all right at the moment, and I'll know if it isn't."

She and Emmi pottered about fetching things, spreading towels on the bed, seeing to the fire now and then and talking quietly to each other, while I cuddled close to Andras. We couldn't talk, with them there, but I wanted them; listening to them chatting so calmly was sort of soothing, and there was so much I wanted to say to Andras that it was simpler to say nothing, especially as I couldn't think of the right words to say it in. And if I could, they would have upset him, particularly the bit that went: please don't let me die because I don't want to leave you.

I had my head buried in his shoulder most of the time, but once when I looked up to kiss him, I saw it was almost full day outside. The dark had gone deep blue, and I could see the magnolia. I couldn't believe how much time had gone by. Well, I thought, I'm doing all right this far.... I leaned back against his arm and smiled, and suddenly there was this tremendous gush; I thought at first it must be blood and I panicked so much, I nearly spoke out loud. Andras's eyes were as wide as mine must have been, but Mum was there in a second.

"It's all right, Andras; it's just the waters broken. It'll be born soon. You'll have to go now."

"Can't I stay? Please?"

He looked stricken. Emmi raised her eyebrows. "Why, of

course, that's what we need; a man standing about in the way fainting.... Makes you wonder why no-one's thought of it before. Out."

Mum hugged him. "Go and keep Marti company, love; he would come, and he'll only worry himself sick. Go and tell him everything's fine."

We hugged and kissed, and he left. In a way it was a good job we couldn't speak, because I could read "goodbye in case" in his eyes, and I suppose he could in mine, and it was hard enough without hearing it.

Mum signed that I should get on the bed, and I heaved myself up there with some help. I felt like an elephant. The pains were a lot worse too, and there hardly seemed to be any gap between them. I was making a lot of noise by now; at first I tried not to, in case he heard it downstairs and got upset, but after a while I couldn't help it. I was sitting up in bed holding my knees, with a blanket over me. I couldn't see what was going on where the baby was, and I didn't care. I'd really changed my mind about having it by this time. Now and again, Mum would say to Emmi that she thought she could just see the head, but even that didn't make me think it'd soon be over. I hadn't thought it was possible to be in this much pain, and now I was, it felt as if there was no reason it should ever end.

I heard a man whistling outside, and then the sound died away down the street. I couldn't believe anyone was going to work as usual, while this was going on. I remember thinking vaguely: Andras'll be late for work, and then: so will Dad... my head really wasn't on straight.

I don't know how long the pain really lasted; I'd lost all track of time, but I remember hearing Emmi's voice, suddenly excited: "There it is!"

"Yes, it's right down. One more push and we'll have hold of it."

I felt like saying "you push", or something a bit less polite, but then there was this unbelievable feeling of being torn apart and I was screaming and Mum was saying: "Now the shoulders..." *and there was another sound, another cry apart from me, and then I pushed again and it was almost as bad but not quite, and then*

suddenly it wasn't. I mean it still hurt, but after that, it was noth-
ing. I thought: I'll never take toothache seriously again.

I knew the baby must be all right, because I could hear Mum
and Emmi laughing and congratulating each other, but it was like
they were the other side of a wall. The first time I was really con-
scious of them was when I had another spasm of pain, and Mum
said: "Here comes the afterbirth. I'll sort it; you give our little
grandson to his mother."

Emmi brought this little white bundle and put it in my arms.
His face looked screwed up and cross, which seemed very under-
standable, but he'd stopped crying. What hair he had was dark,
like mine, but when he opened his eyes he looked more like Andras.
I couldn't get over his tiny little fingers. He was waving them
around as if he wasn't sure what they were for. Emmi put one of
my fingers in his palm, and they folded on it. He mewed, and I
held him closer. I'd changed my mind again, by the way....

Andras and Dad were practically battering the door down. Mum
opened it a crack and said: "He's lovely; you can see him in a
minute but we have to get her tidied up first."

"I don't mind."

I looked a bit panicky at Emmi – I minded him seeing me like
that, and hoped she'd say so for me. But she smiled and gestured
at the baby. I couldn't think what she meant for a moment, and
then suddenly it came to me. I kissed his head, and called out:
"Well, I flaming mind, Andras; you can see us in a minute
when we're presentable. He's beautiful, he looks like you. And
I love you lots and lots. And tell Dad I love him too, and
Auntie" – I could hear her twittering through the door – "and
tell little Jon's grandmothers they're dead clever and I love
them and so does he." And I turned back to the baby:

Puss, chase the mouse
to his little house....

22

Andras; Anni

When I woke, I lay listening to the stillness for a while. Anni had taken him downstairs already, but he must be asleep again, because I couldn't hear her singing. It was bright outside, but I could see raindrops on the glass, and the smells coming in from the garden were damp, like after a spring shower. It felt very quiet. The odd sounds – a bird in the garden, someone's feet on the kitchen floor – just made it stiller, somehow.

Then I heard him wake. He had this little mewing cry; to be perfectly honest I couldn't tell it apart from the cat's at first. But now I knew every tone of his voice, and they all went through me. The mew was when he wasn't unhappy about anything, just awake and wondering what was going on. It never lasted long, because Anni or Mother or Auntie always picked him up.

> The cow sat in the cuckoo's nest
> and taught her lambs to whistle...

I smiled, not so much at the daft words, just at the sound of her singing out loud. I couldn't get enough of it. I loved the way her voice sounded in our room, downstairs, in the garden. I'd always loved it in her house, but now it felt as if it belonged here. When I'd hear her voice drift upstairs, I couldn't believe it hadn't always been there, like the creaky floorboards, or the way the smell of lavender came through the open window in summer.

When I got downstairs, she'd given him to Auntie to hold while she and Mother got breakfast ready. But every time one or other of them came in with something, they'd go over and have a coo at him as well.

"Who's going out today then, eh? Who's going to church with us, to meet all his neighbours?" My mother was dead soft on him. I suppose she must have used that tone of voice to me, at some time, but it was hard to imagine.

"Oh, Daddy and me are going to be ever so proud of you, love. It's a shame about the showers, though, isn't it, on our first day out? Is it going to be warm enough for you out there, pet?"

"Course it will, won't it? You'll be wrapped up all the time, and you're not made of glass; no, you're strong, you are...."

He got talked to all the time, for his own sake and because it was so much easier for them to talk to each other through him than by signs. I often thought it was no wonder he looked permanently puzzled. But if the words didn't mean anything, I suppose the voices did; at any rate he seemed a contented little character.

I remembered when I'd been the only way she could get through to anyone, or they to her. That had been a real strain at times; I'd often enough longed not to have the responsibility of it, and I didn't want it back – at least I didn't think I did... no, nobody could see how happy she was and wish that. But I thought: I'll always remember it. I didn't always want it, but I had it, and I'll never be that much to anyone again.

My mother spared me a glance and went back to her normal tone.

"You're never going to church dressed like that?"

"No, I'll change after breakfast. I'd just rather be comfortable for as long as possible."

Anni kissed me hello. "Can't think what you've got against your good clothes. I love you in them."

"I hate me in them. I feel as if they belong to someone else and I've just dressed up in them. You look great, though."

I went over to say hello to him and Auntie, and she held him out to me. I was still scared stiff of holding him; scared I'd drop him or hold him too tight. It made me as awkward as hell with him, and he generally protested pretty soon. I handed him on to Anni. She seemed to be able to eat, or work, or wander about the house, with him in one arm and never worry about it.

Mealtimes were so different now. With Anni and me able to talk freely, and everyone talking to him, or through him, all the time. It was so carefree, so relaxed; just pure fun. I loved him for that, for having given us her voice back; for looking like her. She used to say he'd set her free. He made a lot of people happy; me too, when I could stop worrying for long enough.

When I went to get changed, she brought him upstairs too, to dress him up in his best stuff – there's something about women that wants men to be uncomfortable from an early age. I took off my work shirt, but she stopped me before I could put the Sunday one on.

"Go and lie down on the bed."

"Eh? With him awake? Anyway there isn't time..."

"Don't be daft! You're scared to hold him, aren't you? If you're on the bed, it won't matter if you do drop him. Sit up a bit. Right."

She'd got him undressed, and she put him on my bare chest and laid his shawl over him. He shivered a bit against me, and I put my hands on him under the shawl. I'd never held him without layers of clothing between us, and it was strange to feel his heart beating against me, stronger than I'd thought it would be. His skin was warm, and I was afraid my hands must feel cold to him, but he didn't seem to mind. He smelt milky and soapy and so clean, so new. I wondered if I still smelt of the yard. I washed every night, but sometimes I felt that awful stink must be ingrained in me by now. Not you, I thought; *you can do better than that.*

He nuzzled against my chest and I could feel his mouth moving and searching, as if he were on Anni. I closed my arms around him without thinking, resting my lips on his head. I didn't feel any less scared or worried about him; in fact I felt the whole world was full of danger for him and I couldn't think how I was going to protect him from all of it. But something did happen, because I wasn't scared about me any more. Well, not *as* scared. I could still get things wrong, I knew that. But I knew I didn't *want* anything but good for him.

When she finally took him off me, it was the first time I'd wanted to hold on to him. I caught her hand.

"Thank you."

"Told you you'd be all right with him."

"You're getting like my mother; she always seems to know me better than I do."

She laughed. "Whose idea do you think it was?"

Emmi tied the shawl for me; across one shoulder and around my waist like a sort of sling. ("The left shoulder, so you can feel your mum's heartbeat, 'cause you like that, don't you, love?") I'd never worn it before; around the house I just carried him, but he fitted in it so snugly and it would keep the showers off him. And it meant I'd got one arm free for Andras.

We set off toward the church, and I grinned up at him. "Twice in four months. I'm getting to be a regular gadabout."

He smiled, but he looked a bit sorry for me.

"It isn't fair, I know. But it'll be a year soon. You'll be able to get out more then."

I hadn't meant it that way, but he's sweet when he gets like that, so I rubbed my face against his shoulder and his hand clenched on my arm. The sun felt warm on my face; it didn't look like rain again just yet, but the showers had brought all the scents out. I could smell damp hyacinths, really strong. And there was the little tree across the road from Mum and Dad's house, covered in white blossom; it was all red berries when we'd last walked this way.

They were all outside the door, waiting for us to catch up. It had taken us an age to get this far, because Susi and Mags and the gang spent so long going "aah" over Jon, while he gazed at them and blew bubbles. My folks had had a few weeks to get used to that, but they were still nearly as bad. All the way to the church, it was the same. Even Jos wanted a go. It was nice to hear his voice again.

"Oh, you're going to have your mum's curls, aren't you? You'd better not turn out as pretty as her, though. When's your dad going to bring you down the yard to meet the lads, then?"

Andras and I smiled at each other. It was odd how often people talked through the baby to him, as well as to me, even though they didn't have to. He was saying, if he got called "your dad" much more often, he'd forget he had a name.

"Don't you dare take him anywhere near the yard, Andras: all those rats.... You'll have to be lots bigger before you go to places like that, won't you, pet?" Never, if I can help it, I thought, and I could see Andras thinking the same, though he wouldn't say it in front of Jos. It's strange how things you accept for yourself suddenly don't seem good enough for them.

There were sheep out on the hills, and I could hear, every so often, some lamb that had wandered away from its mother give that piercing call they have, and the ewe answering it, over and over until they found each other. I'd never noticed what a sharp, painful note lambs' voices have. I thought about all the places you could see from the hills, and how we used to make up stories about what they were like, and dream of going there. I wanted him to go there.

Everyone smiled at him, even the crabby old priest, and even Ossi. I had a hard job not hiding Jon in my shawl from him; I felt like his look might bring bad luck or something. Andras felt the tension through my arm.

"Don't be too hard on him. He hasn't heard a word from Edo since he left."

"Well, I don't suppose he cares. He drove him away."

"Edo was this little once. I can't believe Ossi hated him then."

He was so good all through the service. He slept through the sermon (Andras claimed, afterwards, that it was hardly surprising since he'd slept through most of it himself). He woke up when the Easter hymns started, but he was no trouble. I held him so he could listen to the music and he seemed perfectly happy. I found myself humming behind the veil and stopped, and then realised: *I can: I've got a voice again.* And I started to breathe the words, just loud enough for him to hear.

The morning star against the dawn
I never saw so bright,
Nor ever such a fair spring day
Succeed a winter's night.

143

Afterwards we could barely get out of the church porch for people wanting to meet him; everyone in the village must have said hello. Then we took him round to the graveyard.

"Look, Jon, this is your other grandfather; Daddy's father. He was Jon too: Granny Emmi's Jon. And this is my grand-father, and he was Jon as well, but I called him Bapa."

We'd brought a few flowers; they were drooping a bit after the service, but it was looking like rain again, so with any luck they'd perk up in the open air. We left some on each.

I'd been dreading seeing Bapa's grave for the first time, but it was just a piece of ground. I didn't feel he was *in* there, trapped, longing to be out among us again. And for all I hadn't slept through the sermon, I didn't really feel he was up in the sky looking down, either. But I could feel him; in Nico's big ears, in the baby's name, in everyone who could recall some-thing of him; who could say "remember how he used to...." I thought: I must tell little Jon all that, so he'll go on being here.

When I looked up, I saw Ossi, visiting his wife's grave. Edo's two brothers were there too, but not with him, somehow. He didn't clash with them like he had with Edo, but there wasn't much closeness either. I saw him look at the grave, and at them, and then across to us, and his face said: who'll visit mine? You could see he was wondering if they'd head off to the city too; if they'd ever bring his grandsons back.

Well, he had himself to blame if they didn't. But Andras was right after all; you could feel sorry for someone even then. If he was that way made, that there wasn't enough kindness in him to make his own sons care for him; if there was nothing they wanted their children to know about him, then he was really going to die. I wondered how I could ever have felt alone.

23

EDO

Thirty-seven people live in this building. The landlord's agent told me, when he last came round for the rent. Most of them wouldn't know me to look at. The ones on this floor, maybe; we give each other a quick nod as we pass in the corridors. There's an oldish woman next on the left; she came to my door one day with a jar; the lid was too stiff for her fingers, and I opened it for her. On the right there's a woman with three children; I don't know where the husband is. She apologised to me once on the stairs, because the children make such a racket sometimes. I said it didn't bother me. Across the landing there's a tall, fair-haired man, a labourer, I think – I saw him coming in on a hot day once, with his shirt off, and his shoulders were all muscle. He goes out early and comes back late; I hardly see him. I haven't really noticed any of the rest.

And in this street there are forty-eight houses. It's off a much longer street, with trees each side and a lot of traffic, where the numbers go into the hundreds. I walked down it once, and into the next, and the next, and the next, until I was lost. I just walked and walked; I must have passed hundreds of people, and none of them knew me. I'd force myself to look into their faces, and there was nothing there. No knowledge, no expectation. I felt so happy, I could have walked all day.

Back home, I never looked into a face without seeing someone who knew me, and what to expect from me. *Oh, Edo's got two left feet. He's crap at games; useless with his hands; can't look anyone in the eye; weird, something wrong about him; everyone knows that....*

To get to work, I walk halfway down the street with forty-eight houses, then a little way down the very long street, then across it and down a short winding lane with shops that leads into a longish, wide road with offices and warehouses. It's early in the morning; there are plenty of people about but they're all going to work, same as me, and they aren't really thinking about much else. If you steal a look at their faces, there's something not quite alive in them yet, as if they've only woken up as much of themselves as they needed to get their feet moving.

I work in one of the warehouses. It's a big grocery warehouse; I weigh out dry goods like flour and salt and such, and bag them up for delivery. They supply half the city. I have to keep the records of what's gone where, too, and what's been lost to the rats.

When I first came to town, I worked a few streets farther off, in one of the mills. It was the strangest place. Nobody could really talk while they were working – the overseers didn't like it for one thing, but anyway you couldn't hear a word above the power looms and the belts of the machinery on the go all the time. And yet they were talking all the time, in signs or reading each other's lips. The girls were brilliant at it. I remember one time, I got a broken thread and I said something really foul under my breath, and two women opposite nearly choked themselves laughing. I was ready to die, but they just said they'd heard worse. Actually they probably *used* worse; they were a rough bunch, but a lot of them were nice to me. To them I was this wide-eyed lad from the country who needed looking after. They'd chat to me in the break; ask me all about myself, and I'd tell them, though I made most of it up.

I left there after about a month. Nobody thought that odd; most of the men left as soon as they could get anything better, because the pay was lousy. Some of the women stayed for years – I suppose for them, it wasn't such bad money – but even they'd move on if they found a better place. That's how it is here; people move on all the time. From one room to another; you often see a cart outside our building with someone's bits and pieces on it. Or another job. I've been in the warehouse a couple of months now, and people have come and gone in that time.

It's not like joining some sort of family or club, using your dad's tools, signing up for life. It's more like dropping into something for a while, something that changes shape all the time, that people belong to for a while and then not any more. It's like being born again each time.

It feels quiet in the warehouse, early in the morning, but then anywhere would after the mill. Sometimes, coming home, I'd see the older women still lip-reading as they chatted, and I thought it was habit till I realised all that clatter had damaged their hearing. It's all men here; I miss the gossip a bit. About half a dozen of us bagging up; we nod to each other and get on with it, because if the stuff isn't ready when the carts come round, the delivery men give you a cursing. They've got no patience at all, but I suppose they get cursed too, if they're late at the shops. Everything happens so fast here. When I think of a piece of hide lying around that yard for more than a year, turning into leather, it seems like another world.

I know some of the carters a bit now, as much as I need to; which ones'll give you a good word for having things ready; which ones give you hell for being half a minute late, and then take it out on their horses. They're a rowdy lot, compared to the warehousemen. It always seems quiet when they've left, though there's still plenty to do. I know the warehousemen by name too, now. Matt, Daniel, Christoph... no, he left last week. They're all right, as far as I know.

To them, I'm the bloke who keeps himself to himself and doesn't jump two feet in the air if he sees a rat. They've got them here, of course, and some of the men really get the horrors when they scurry out suddenly. I don't like them any better than most folk, but you can't talk about being infested with rats until you've worked in a tanyard; they're running over your feet there, even with all the dogs around. They use traps here.

In the break, you might read the paper; a couple of the married men chat about their families maybe, or the young ones about a dance or a match. But a lot of us don't know each other outside work anyway, living in different parts of town. Work's what you do for however many hours you have to, then you go home and forget it; become someone else.

Sometimes in the break, I go down to the river; it isn't far. It isn't like any river I've ever seen; it carries as much traffic as the roads do. The boats and barges go up and down all day, and the boatmen curse and shout worse than the carters. They laugh a lot too, though, and even now, when it's hardly summer yet, their faces and arms are brown all over. They're like knotted rope, those arms; I can't imagine how strong they must be.

I could watch them all day. To be carried on a river; never seeing the same landscape for more than a few moments; never staying in one place long enough to make a mess of things... no wonder they look happy.

There's a big market on the quayside; sometimes they send one of us down there to check who's giving good value for what, or maybe complain if the weight was short last time, or the sugar was mouldy. I do all right. I'm not scared of anyone, when I know I won't ever have to see them again if I don't want.

Or you might be checking stock, or bagging up again – it goes on all day, though the busy time is early morning – making sure the place is kept swept, nothing around that can start a fire, or maybe sifting things out of the flour that shouldn't have got in there – that's a laugh, because the shopkeepers will probably just put it back in. I know where half the dust on shop floors ends up. It's all right; it's a job. I might stay on, for a while anyway. At least I smell clean, these days. It took two weeks out of that tanyard, before I stopped feeling I stank.

On the way home, I stop at one of the shops in the lane and buy some food. A widow runs it; she's got a soft spot for me ever since she found out I live on my own. She's always asking if I'm looking after myself and eating properly; she'd give me extra weight if I didn't stop her. I quite like her fussing over me, but I don't want to owe her.

I love the evenings here. Now the weather's warm enough, you can wander the streets till dark and beyond it, and they're always crowded. People shopping late after work, or just looking in the windows at what they can't afford. Or listening to bands in the park, or fiddlers on the pavement. Dressed up for the theatre or the concert, or sitting outside the cafes watching everyone else walk by.... And when it's dark, the lights are so bright, you can hardly see the stars.

I've got some good clothes. I don't mean my Sunday stuff from home; these are things you could wear in an office. I bought them as soon as I could scrape enough money together after paying the rent – that was one time I really wasn't eating properly. Of course the widow hasn't seen them, nor anyone at work. I go out in them some evenings; just walk around catching sight of myself in shop windows and seeing someone else, someone I don't know.

One evening a week, I go to the night school. That's another set of people I don't see anywhere else.... I'm learning accounts, as far as the teacher's concerned. He doesn't know what else. He's a retired clerk, quite elderly, with silver hair and smooth, white hands, like you have when you've never worked with them. And this voice. It's really beautiful, his voice, calm and low and sort of *refined*, somehow. I'm learning it. Every time he says something different – differently – from how I would, I make a note. I practise in front of a mirror in my room, making my lips form the same shapes his do, over and over until the sounds come out the same.

When I bought the clothes, the shopman looked as if he thought I'd stolen the money. Even now, I can't wear them and speak, because everyone would know what I really was. But when I've got this voice right, and a few other things, I can be who I like.

I know that's possible; I've seen it. The most fantastic thing that's happened to me since I came here was the first night I went to the theatre. I'd seen players at home now and then, sure, people dressed up in school or at some fair. But that was all it ever was: people I knew, dressed up. This was so different. It was dark, for one thing; I'll never forget when they turned the lights down, so that I and everyone around me was lost in shadows and whispers and all I could see was the stage. I got shivers all through me, I was so excited. And then this actor came on and played some hero character, some general, I think, who wanted to be the emperor or something. I didn't understand half the words, to be honest, but I understood *him*; his longings, his loneliness when nobody else felt what he did; the way he felt lifted when the soldiers cheered him; the way he felt betrayed. I really believed in him. And then at the end, when the lights came on, this actor came forward and I was struck dumb. He was about an inch shorter than me, and I'd have sworn he was three inches taller. He'd looked so handsome, so distinguished, when he was being the general, but he had an ordinary, mousy sort of face, and when I saw it in the light, even under the paint, I could see he was much younger than he'd made his voice sound.

You'd think I'd have been disappointed: maybe I was at first, when I realised the general wasn't there any more. But if I was, it didn't last long. I've been back a couple of times since. I'd go every night, if I could afford it, but I found the bar where the actors drink and I sit there sometimes, in the shadows so the landlord won't notice how long I make a drink last, and listen to them. Most of the time they sound as ordinary as me, but now and then one of them will put on an old-man voice, or a foreign accent, or pretend to be dying or in love. And for as long as it lasts, it's real; they can slip out of one skin and into another like changing a suit. Whoever they started off as, they can be anyone they want to be.

24

Anni; Hanna

Jon slept late for once; when he woke me it was already light, and Andras was nowhere to be seen. I was amazed; him waking before me was something to mark in the calendar.... Even that thought didn't remind me. I was just rocking Jon, feeding him, singing to him, listening to rain on the window and thinking it was a good thing, because we'd had a dry spell and the garden could do with it.... And he came in, with a huge bunch of forget-me-nots.

"What are those for... oh, of course!"

It was the seventeenth of May: it was a year exactly. I couldn't believe I'd forgotten. Andras and I had been talking about it for days; we'd even mentioned it last night, and yet by this morning it had gone clean out of my head. He laughed.

"Well, I thought it'd mean more to you than that!"

"It does; it does.... Hang on while he finishes. There now.... Go to Daddy, love, while I sort these. Aren't they pretty, then? They'll shed all over the floor, as it happens, but never mind; I'll put something down to catch them, later. There. How late is it?"

"Breakfast's ready."

"Never! He must really have slept in. I'd better get dressed. Do you want me to put him back in his crib?"

"No, he's all right."

I got dressed as usual, a bit quickly maybe, because I was embarrassed about sleeping late. I glanced in the mirror to check everything was all right, and then suddenly I realised what I didn't need, and I took the silver coat off again. I folded it carefully and went to put it away in a drawer. But Andras reached out first and touched it. He had a strange look on his face.

"What's the matter; will you miss it? I won't; it's starting to look dead scruffy."

"I love whatever you wear. But you won't throw it away, will you?"

"No, of course not. I'll get some paper, later, and store it properly. Hey, aren't you going to be late for work?"

"Your dad said I could come in a bit late if I make it up. I can take you over there tonight; think about that."

"I know... I can hardly believe it. I feel like dragging you round all the aunties and uncles, everywhere I'm allowed to go – don't look so horrified; I won't really! Not if you promise we can take Jon out in the woods next Sunday if it's fine. Just us."

By the time we got downstairs, Emmi had all the work done. She raised an eyebrow, but I knew her face, and it wasn't annoyed. I signed "sorry", and then remembered what else had changed today.... But she was quicker.

"Welcome back."

"Haven't been away." I gave her the baby to say hello to, and she cooed over him at some length.

Auntie pattered over from her chair and gave me something wrapped in tissue, signing "anniversary present" and "careful". I opened it very gently and it was one of her birds' eggs, some sort of duck by the look of it, with all sorts of clasped hands and chain-link patterns on it and an opening in front – how she managed to cut holes in them without breaking them I couldn't think, but she'd got very good at it. Inside, through the opening, you could see two figures cut out of card, a little man and woman, holding hands.

I was dead touched; it must have taken her ages. I said: "Andras, look at this; isn't it brilliant?" and he and Emmi agreed, and I kissed Auntie and signed "thank you". She was the only person left in the house that I couldn't speak to, now, and somehow it made me feel sorry for her, as if she were the one on the edge. Daft, really, because she was still the one who could go anywhere and speak to anyone; she certainly wasn't short of gossip. But I still thought: I must talk to her through Jon more.

When I saw Andras off to work, he said: "I won't be late back. I'll make the time up working through my break. We'll go over and see your folks straight after tea. They've got a surprise for you." He wouldn't tell me any more; just grinned and walked off.

"Do you know what it is?" I asked Emmi.

"Yes." She smiled too, but I could see I wasn't going to get any more out of her. I wondered if Mum would come round. She wasn't as good at keeping secrets as Emmi.

It was a very normal sort of day, considering. So many times, over the last year, I'd thought: I wish I could say this to Emmi, or ask her about that, and I'd thought that when I could, it would be like a dam bursting. Yet now I couldn't recall most of the things I'd stored up, or there didn't seem to be a need for them any more. While Jon was awake, we spent most of the time talking to him, or about him, just as usual.

"Andras swears you were never as soft with him."

"Does he? I was when he was this age, I think. Later... well, maybe not. I had to be other things too. Well, I couldn't say "wait till your father gets home", could I?"

I laughed. "I don't think I'll be able to, either! Can you see Andras coming over all stern?"

"No, not really.... What did you do with all those forget-me-nots he brought in?"

"Oh, I forgot! They're in a jug upstairs, but I ought to put some paper down or they'll shed all over the carpet; they're pretty nearly blown. I'll go and do it now."

"Ah, don't worry about it; they won't do it any harm. The sun's coming through; we could take him out in the garden while it's fine. It'll be nice next year, when you and I can go out together with him."

"It's so difficult sometimes, remembering what I'm allowed to do when, and who with."

"I know. It's amazing, the things we invent to make life harder. You know, I don't suppose it would bother Andras if you just stopped doing all this? Some folk would talk, yes, but he could stand that if you could."

"I can't. I've thought about it, lots of times, but I can't just not do it. I don't know why. Mum did it, and my grans and my aunties, and you, and... I think about that a lot; it makes me mad when someone like Gina says it was all pointless, even if it was... I don't want to be the first not to. It isn't exactly that I'm scared of what people would think – well, perhaps it is, partly – but it's more that a bit of me would think it too. I'm just not brave, I suppose."

After tea, when we were getting ready to go out, (with Andras still grinning all over his face and refusing to tell me anything), Emmi said maybe she shouldn't come.

"Why? You haven't had a row with Mum, have you?"

"When did anyone last manage to have a row with your mother? I'm just not sure it's a good idea today. She's got another year to wait, remember."

"I hadn't thought about it like that... but come on, she didn't get ratty with Andras when I could talk to him. Please come, Emmi; I'll be tactful and not keep talking to you all the time. She probably won't notice anyone except Jon anyway."

I tried to recall if we'd moved anything, changed anything. I wanted the place to be as near as it could to how she'd remember it. As if she'd never been away.

But of course, the one thing I couldn't put back as it used to be was her. The woman who walked into the house wasn't the Anni who used to live here, the girl with long black curls down to her waist who was always singing or scrapping with her sister or consoling someone like Edo, and who didn't have a care in the world unless one of the cats was ill. I could still sense that girl in the house, like a happy ghost: I sometimes felt she was behind me, and I'd see her if I could only turn round fast enough.

She looked round, smiled, touched things, pointed things out to Andras that she'd missed or remembered, but all the time you could see it was somewhere she *used* to live, and didn't any more. Once, when she'd touched a picture, she straightened it up afterwards, as Emmi would have done. Only when the cats strolled in, and she ran to pick them up; then it was her as she used to be. But then she turned to Andras and said "Isn't this one like our Sooty?"

I'd been too busy to go over during the day, so I hadn't had to watch her talking to Emmi yet. It was only when I saw them together that I realised how much I'd been dreading it. But strangely enough, they hardly exchanged a word for ages. I thought at first they must have had a row, but they both looked quite cheerful. Then I thought maybe they were trying to spare my feelings, and I wished I felt more grateful.

Then Andras picked Jon up, and I said something about how good he was with him – he was, too; he held him so lovingly, not at arm's length like some men do – and Anni and Emmi glanced at each other at the same time and smiled about some private joke, and it all at once came over me that they'd been doing that, talking with their faces and minds ever since they came in; they didn't speak because they didn't need to. And for the first time ever, I felt really angry with this whole business that had taken her away from me and brought her so close to someone else, while I had to stand by and watch, not able to do anything about it. I felt like crying or screaming, and I invented an errand in the kitchen to get out of the way for a moment; get control of myself. Everyone was making such a fuss of Jon, even the lads; I knew it wouldn't be noticed if I were gone for a bit.

I was chopping some vegetables, when a hand caught my wrist.

"If you cut them in that mood," Emmi said, "you're going to lose a couple of fingers. Anyway I bet you don't need to do any more. You'd be better off saying what you feel."

"I don't have anything to say."

"All right then, I will. It's very unfair that you have to wait a year longer than me to talk to the lass, and you're fed up about it. I certainly would be. Same as I get fed up because Andras finds it easier to talk to you than he does to me."

"Why, that's not... I've never...."

"Oh, don't be daft; you *are* easier; if I'm not, it's my fault. I should be grateful to you for being there to listen to him – I am, sometimes. That doesn't stop me getting mad about it now and then. It's allowed, you know. And *you* don't really want Anni to pine for you and her old home... only, a bit of you does. Go on, say it."

"I... I'm really glad she's happy, and that you two get on so well. I remember not getting on with my mother-in-law. But... yes, I feel miserable because I'm not first with her any more, and by the time I can talk to her again she won't need me because she'll be yours instead and... and I can still sense her around here as she was, but now she's moved on and... oh, damn everything. Damn it. Damn it."

Emmi laughed softly. "Strongest language I ever heard you use. You should have tried some of that on old Kati; she'd have taken better to it than she did to you biting everything back."

"You don't know some of what I would have said to her, if I hadn't. People can spend their lives regretting things they've said."

"What about things they haven't said? When Adam was crying his eyes out at the funeral, do you suppose it was because of the rows he and the old man had when he was young – or all those years later, when they barely said a word? I've thought about that a lot, since. You know, *you* say things to Andras – just normal, nice, kind things – that I was always too embarrassed to say, even if I thought them. I used to think it was nice that we could nearly always tell what the other one was thinking without words anyway, but that isn't all they're for, is it... I don't know if I could, even now, but I might have to try."

"I'm sorry if you thought I was trying to take him away from you."

"No... not when I was thinking straight. Look at them."

I glanced through the door into the main room. Anni was holding Jon, and Andras had his arm around her. They were like a little circle that everyone else was on the edge of.

As I watched, they both happened to look round and said, at exactly the same moment: "Where's Mum?" Emmi and I had a fit of the giggles and had to compose ourselves before we went in.

Anni tugged his sleeve. "Andras, when do I find out about this surprise thing? I'm dying to know."

He grinned at me. "Well, you know the singer comes back tomorrow?"

"Yes. So?"

"Three weeks later than usual?"

"Is it? I suppose so... but so what?"

"It's so you can go. You can even sing, now."

Her face lit up. "What! No, hang on... I can't go to just any house yet, even with you; only kinfolk's houses."

"That's why it'll be here. Your mum and dad swapped with the folks who were going to do it."

"Though if her dad had known all his things were going to be tidied up so he could never find them again," put in Marti, "he might have thought twice about it."

She flew over and hugged him, and me, laughing with pure pleasure, and then went back to tell Jon how much she loved everybody. Her eyes were absolutely alight, and everyone's face they rested on seemed to light up too, as if she'd held a candle to it.

25

THE SINGER; ANNI

I wish there weren't so many dogs in this house. I don't mind the cats so much; they keep themselves to themselves, but dogs all think you want to be their friend. I can't think why; I've given them no cause, but that's dogs for you: too thick to take a hint. Actually I think there's only two. They just gallop around enough for a pack.

The folks are kind, though – the woman can't talk to me, of course, but she fed me well and then left me alone to rest, which I appreciate; when I've been on the road all day, the last thing I want to do is tell a bunch of strangers all about the last place I was in. I sat in the shade by the fountain with my hat over my eyes, pretending to snooze whenever someone peered out, and listening to the kitchen fill up with women's voices. Helping with the food, they'd say. Well, the married women are helping with the gossip, and the girls spend more time playing with the cats than anything else.

In the end, it got too lively even to pretend sleep, and I came in and started tuning my guitar. The girls were upstairs by now, doing their hair or whatever but still making an almighty racket, and folk were arriving from other houses. It's odd how they sort themselves into groups for these things; they'll arrive as a family, but then the wife goes over to the married women, the men all stick together, the children make a little zoo of their own, and the lads and lasses cluster separately and then spend all evening gazing across at each other. Same wherever you go.

Naturally there's a bit of interchange. When the girls come down, they stay in little knots at first and eye the boys, but pretty soon, some of them wander over to the women's side to gush over the babies. Of course, that means the boys can watch them walking, as well. There's one very small baby, still wrapped up in a shawl; I can hardly see it, but the girls are making almost as much fuss as if it were a kitten.

One of them straightens up, and I know that long fall of dark hair and the quizzical smile, from last October. *Yes!* Still free, still singing, still refusing to come down. I have a moment of pure happiness and it must show in my face. She smiles back, cooler than I did and with raised eyebrows, but she looks amused, not offended. Come to think about it, I'm not sure which is worse. How old do I look to her?

They're all sitting down now, falling quiet. I strike up something easy, something they can do the work on while I settle in. It's got a long, slow rhythm; I see the women rocking their babies to it, breathing the words under their veils. You can just hear them sometimes, very low and sweet, and it drives me mad because I can't hear more. *Sing out; sing for me as well as him. Sing for you.* Thank God for my girls.

One of the women sets a baby girl on the floor; it's just starting to crawl. Its little cap comes off, and the hair colour nearly makes me miss a note: it's that glinting red from a year and a half back, I'd know it anywhere.... I look at the woman, what there is of her to look at, trying to see Rowanhair. But there's just the eyes, and how can I ever know? Any one of these might be one of mine. I haven't forgotten Redlips yet. Red hair, black curls, pretty mouths, sweet voices that aren't for strangers any more.

I wish I'd gone blind before I saw
her body like snow, her curling hair,
before my life was too hard to bear.

Pity the man who sees her face,
and pity the man who never has,
and all who cannot see her always.

I wish I were blind, old man, like you.
I used to pity the great sorrow
of sightless eyes. I do not now.

I don't usually get maudlin so quick. The men liked that, though. Who knows, we might get away without *Blackweir River*....

I visit this house most days, now. *My home,* I used to call it. The place I'd lived in all my life.

It doesn't feel any different, but I do. I feel like someone who lived here, not like someone who lives here now. When I go into the kitchen to help, it's as a guest might, waiting to be shown what to do, not like someone who knows where things go – I don't, anyway; Mum or Ria seems to have reorganised things.

The animals all know me though, as if I'd never been away. I love that about them, the way their feelings don't change. You can't help wishing it could be like that with other things sometimes – that a choirboy could keep his voice, or a place stay the same for ever, or someone not grow old. It wouldn't work, though.

Last time I was at one of these, I spent most of the time looking over at Andras and thinking about him. I don't feel any differently about that. Yes, I do. More. Some of the looking then was for the girls' benefit, because we all wanted to have someone we could call our own; it was like a sort of badge of achievement. It's all for me, now. He looks at me, and moves his lips very slightly in a kiss. I give it back with my eyes, as well as I can.

Emmi, beside me, raises an eyebrow and murmurs: "Still think he's perfect, then?"

"Not perfect. But as good as I want. As good as anyone could want."

"Mm. Yes, he *is*, actually. Maybe I should tell him so some-time. Do you think it would make him insufferable?"

I laughed. A lot of the things we say to each other don't seem to need answers, or we know the answers already.

The singer strikes up again. He's singing the crane song with Ria. He sang that with me, the last time I ever sang for strangers. I can't take my eyes off them. They sing well together – no, great; that song's never choked me up so much before. I'm aching with it; I don't dare sing it soft behind the veil, in case I let myself go. Afterwards, under the applause, Emmi asks: "Do you miss all that?"

"Yes. Yes, I do. I don't feel that was me any more; it's like

160

it happened to someone else. But I do miss her. Same as you miss the child who used to sledge down hills or climb trees, or the girl the boys used to fancy. Where do all those folk *go*, do you think?"

"Don't know. Change into something else, I suppose. You can't stop yourself changing – well, unless you keep moving from place to place like that fellow. He never seems to change from year to year, but then he doesn't stay long enough for anyone or anywhere to change him."

"Yes, he's odd, isn't he? He's there, and yet part of him isn't. I suppose it comes of not belonging anywhere. *He* always looks as if he's got half his mind on the last place he came from or the next one he's going to. I wonder sometimes if he ever sees anywhere properly."

"Or anyone. You know, I've never heard him ask after anyone? And yet he's been here often enough, twice a year for God knows how long; you'd think he'd have struck up something by now. That there'd be someone he remembered and thought kindly of, from one season to another. But he doesn't even keep names in his head."

"Ssh, he's starting again."

She's good now, my little star. As good a voice as I recall. And not back to earth yet.... There's a boy making sheep's eyes at her, but I can't remember if it's the same one who was doing it in October. Well; it didn't work then; why should it now? *Who would choose bonds, when they had none?* Most folk, actually, but maybe she's different. Maybe she's like me.

But nothing comes for nothing. She might be able to see through the boys, but she isn't exactly besotted with me, either. She's got that cool, amused smile, and when it's aimed at the boys it's fine, but sometimes I think she's just as amused by me. She comes in on time because she's a musician, not because her eyes are fixed on mine; she sings for her, not me. Isn't that what I say I want?

I think of that town miss last year, whose look said *how quaint*. Christ, am I losing it?

I'll never forget when Redlips sang that song with me. I

don't think her voice was any better than Magpie's is now, but there was something between us; we had a real understanding. I wonder if it was just then, just for as long as the music lasted? I'm sure it was more than that. The way she acted the words, became the crane... I don't care how much she loved that lad; there was something of that in her; something that wanted to be up and gone.

Where is she now; dressed just like all the others; with that man who was just like all the others; nursing a baby just like all the others? How can she stand that? Living in the same place year in, year out, with people who never change? Buried before you're dead, girl.

> When I'm walking on down the track
> I keep looking forward: I don't look back.
>
> I say hello; I say goodbye.
> Goodbye comes easier; I don't know why.
>
> Nail my boots to the kitchen floor;
> I'll walk barefoot out of the door,
>
> Sun, come out and melt this snow:
> Don't want footprints when I go.
>
> Me and my shadow, all alone;
> I'll give him the slip, some day soon.

I don't recall that one.... I wonder if he made it up? Edo would have liked it. I wonder how he's doing in the city. All those people who don't know him.... It's scary to think this man might have passed him in the street and never known.

I've never understood anyone less than I do this man. Edo... well, I knew what made him the way he was, and I don't think he ever *wanted* to be like that. He hung around the edge of people; he was just so afraid to get close to them. You see a cat, sometimes, that's timid with people; it'll just let you stroke it with a fingertip maybe, and then it backs off. But you can see it would *like* to come close and be stroked, if it only dared.

But him... he's more like a fox or a wild bird, that won't come close at all. One of the girls is trying to talk to him now, they generally do when he's between songs. Because when he's singing he links eyes, and it's like he's singing just for you, and you'd swear he was in love. But that's all acting, just the words of the songs. When they talk to him he flirts; makes out they're breaking his heart, but you can tell that's acting too, it's his way of keeping them at arm's length.

It's fun to act in a song, to be someone else for a while. I wouldn't want to do it all the time, though. All those different voices and none of them yours.... When I had no voice, I was scared because I wasn't sure what it would be, when I got it back again.

Jon's wide awake. I'm sure he likes the music. But I suppose all the attention's fun, too. Mum's holding out her arms for him, so I hand him over for a bit.

"Oh, you are so gorgeous; you're going to be as beautiful as your mother when she was little...."

I used to feel a bit pushed out at first, when she cooed over him so much, but I know now that a lot of what she says to him is for me too. Like Emmi says soft things to him that she really means for Andras.

He starts to whimper and his mouth's moving as if he's hungry. Mum gives him straight back and I take him out to the kitchen – fortunately the singer's still taking a rest, so we're not interrupting anything. Hard luck if we were, though.

It hurts a bit, when he feeds. You wouldn't think a little mouth could be so strong. It's such a strange feeling; it takes from me, but I want it to. I want *him* to. The only time I've ever felt anything like it was singing in a crowd, and even that wasn't quite it.

When Ria was singing, I remembered last year, feeling: *this is me, just me and nobody else*. Well, you feel that when it's your voice soaring, but if you think about it, I suppose it can't be. Nobody's born alone. Your folks make you what you are, and then everyone else who comes along changes you a bit.... I can hear some of Emmi in my voice now, and him, and something that was never there before when I speak to Jon.

The kitchen door opens and I reach for my shawl, but it's only Andras.

"Got bored without you both." He sits down beside us and puts his arm around me, and I lean on it, resting – it does your back in, feeding. The pull is gentler now; Jon's going to sleep. I'll unlatch him soon, but we might as well make sure. I start crooning to him, very softly, and Andras joins in as well. They won't hear us next door; the singer's struck up again.

NOTE

The genesis of this novel was a passage in *Essays in the Study of Folk-Songs* by the Countess Evelyn Martinengo-Cesaresco, published by J.M. Dent, 1886. She was discussing Armenian marriage customs:

> [The bride] has not uttered a single word save when alone with her husband since she pronounced the marriage vow. She may not hope to do so till after the birth of her first-born child; then she will talk to her nursling, after a while to her mother-in-law, some time later she may converse with her own mother, and by-and-by.... with the young girls of the house.

There was more, about the details of the custom, its rationale and effects.

I have no idea whether the Countess's assertions were correct, and have no wish to find out – you can ruin a good story by checking out the facts. I wanted to write a 'what if', about custom and communication and the way they socialise some folk and not others: a story of choirs and lone voices. I didn't, particularly, set it in Armenia or 1886, either. The names are as little located as possible; they mostly have a vaguely East European feel but are intended to be as universal as they can be. The tanyard is from rural Wales and could have existed anywhere suitable in Europe at any time from the Middle Ages to the early twentieth century – the process changed remarkably little. Some of the folk-songs are invented, but heavily reliant on common folk-motifs, others are quoted or reconstructed from all over the place (Armenia, Wales and Iceland, among others). In two cases they owe a debt to named writers: the song 'I wish I'd gone blind' in chapter 25 is adapted from three verses by the Irish Gaelic poet Uilliam Ruadh (16th-17th century), and the 'Easter hymn' in chapter 22, "The morning star..." is an intentional mistranslation of the opening of a seventeenth-century German hymn by Friedrich Spee von Langenfeld, *Die reine stirn der morgenroth*. A true translation of the first two lines would be "the pure brow of dawn was never so well ornamented". And the lines from 'When Adam was in Paradise' in chapter 17 are direct quotes from an old Irish carol, but have no named author that I know of.